KASHMIR
BY
SIR FRANCIS YOUNGHUSBAND

PREFACE

When Major Molyneux asked me to combine with him in the production of a book on Kashmir I could not resist the temptation to describe what he had so faithfully depicted, though my official duties naturally leave me insufficient time to do real justice to the theme. I have not been able to write with the completeness that I should have wished; and I am aware of many sins of omission. I can only hope that when the description fails the reader will be fortunate to have his attention irresistibly diverted to one or other of my collaborator's beautiful pictures.

THE RESIDENCY, SRINAGAR,
September 1908.

CHAPTER I
SCENERY AND SEASONS

Bernier, the first European to enter Kashmir, writing in 1665, says: "In truth, the kingdom surpasses in beauty all that my warmest imagination had anticipated." This impression is not universally felt, for one of the very latest writers on Kashmir speaks of it as overrated, and calls the contour of the mountains commonplace and comparable to a second-rate Tyrolean valley. And fortunate it is that in this limited earth of ours we every one of us do not think alike. But I have seen many visitors to Kashmir, and my experience is that the bulk of them are of the same view as the above-mentioned Frenchman. They have read in books, and they have heard from friends, glowing descriptions of the country; but the reality has, with most, exceeded the expectation. Some have found the expenses of living and the discomforts of travel greater than they had expected. And some have arrived when it was raining or cloudy, and the snows were not visible; or in the middle of summer when the valley is hazy, steamy, and filled with mosquitoes. But when the clouds have rolled by, the haze lifted, and a real Kashmir spring or autumn day disclosed itself, the heart of the hardest visitor melteth and he becomes as Bernier.

The present book will deal, not with the whole Kashmir State, which includes many outlying provinces, but with Kashmir Proper, with the world-renowned valley of Kashmir, a saucer-shaped vale with a length of 84 miles, a breadth of 20 to 25 miles, and a mean height of 5600 feet above sea-level, set in the very heart of the Himalaya, and corresponding in latitude to Damascus, to Fez in Morocco, and to South Carolina.

APPROACH TO SRINAGAR

The country with which one is most apt to compare it is, naturally, Switzerland. And Switzerland, indeed, has many charms, and a combination of lake and mountain in which, I think, it excels Kashmir. But it is built on a smaller scale. There is not the same wide sweep of snow-clad mountains. There is no place where one can see a complete *circle* of snowy mountains surrounding a plain of anything like the length and breadth of the Kashmir valley, for the main valleys of Switzerland are like the side valleys of Kashmir. And above everything there is not behind Switzerland what there is at the back of Kashmir, and visible in glimpses from the southern side,—a region of stupendous mountains surpassing every other in the world.

By these Himalayan regions only, by the mountains of Baltistan and Hunza, and by those unequalled mountains seen from Darjiling, can Kashmir be excelled. There indeed one sees mountain majesty and sublimity at their very zenith. And with such as these Kashmir cannot compare. But it possesses a combination of quiet loveliness and mountain grandeur which has a fascination all its own. If one could imagine the smiling, peaceful Thames valley with a girdle of snowy mountains, he would have the nearest approach to a true idea of Kashmir it is possible to give. He would not expect the stern ruggedness and almost overwhelming majesty of the mighty mountains beyond Kashmir. But he would have the tranquil beauty and genial loveliness which to some are even preferable.

Of this, my collaborator's pictures will give a true and vivid impression, though every artist allows that it is impossible to give in a single picture the broad general effect of those wide-flung landscapes and of the snowy ranges stretching from one horizon to another. For that impression and for the varying effect of spring and autumn, of winter and summer, dependence must be on the pen alone.

Which is the most lovely season each must decide for himself. In the spring we think the spring the most exquisitely beautiful. In the autumn we say that nothing could exceed the charm of the brilliant autumn tints. But as it is in the spring that most visitors first arrive, and as it is the real beginning of the year, there will be some advantage in commencing in that season the delicate task of describing Kashmir.

In the first week in March I drove into Kashmir,—this last year, fortunately, in fine weather. In other years at this season I might not have been so fortunate, and the reader must take this possibility of drenching rain, of muddy roads, and dangerous landslips into account. For that purpose, however, there is no need to offer aid to his imagination, as rainy days are much the same all the world over.5

THE LAND OF ROSES

The long drive from the Railway Station at Rawal Pindi, 196 miles from Srinagar, was nearly ended. We had steadily ascended the valley of the Jhelum, with the river continually dashing past us on the left, a strong impetuous stream now being turned to useful ends, firstly, in generating electric power near Rampur, and secondly, in irrigating millions of acres in the plains of the Punjab below. We had passed through the peaceful deodar forest on either side of Rampur, and the splendid limestone cliffs which rise precipitously from them. Just beyond we had passed massive ruins of the so-called Buddhist, but really Hindu temple, dating about 700 A.D. All the country had been blanketed with snow; the hill-sides forested with thousands of Christmas trees glistening in the brilliant sunshine, and the frozen road had been rattling under the ponies' feet. When gradually the narrow valley opened out. The enclosing hills widened apart. The river from a rushing torrent became as placid as the Thames, with numerous long-prowed boats gliding smoothly downward. The little town of Baramula, and the first distinctive chalet-like, but dirty, shaky habitations of Kashmir; a graceful Hindu temple; fine specimens of the famous 6chenar trees; and a typical log bridge, came into view; and then, as the hill-sides finally parted asunder, the glorious valley itself—a valley on so extensive a scale as really to be a plain amidst the mountains—was disclosed; and faintly mingling with the cloudless azure of the sky, on the far side stretched the great range of snowy mountains which bound Kashmir on the north, with the Haramokh peak, 16,900 feet high, standing boldly out 35 miles distant immediately in front; and from just beyond Baramula even Nanga Parbat itself, 26,600 feet, and 70 miles distant, towering nobly over the lower ranges, the solitary representative of the many mountain giants which lay behind.

Then as we emerged into the open valley the snow disappeared and the first faint signs of spring were visible. All the trees were indeed still bare. Neither on the massive chenar nor on the long lines of poplars which bordered the road continuously from Baramula to Srinagar was there a vestige of a leaf; and all the grass was absolutely brown. But in the willows there was just the suspicion of yellow-green. The little leaf-buds were just preparing to burst. On the ground were frequent masses of yellow crocuses and familiar bluebells. Here and 7there were clumps of violets. Occasionally a tortoise-shell or cabbage-white butterfly would flutter by. Above all, the glorious brilliant sunshine, the open, clear blue sky, and the soft touch and gentle feel which at noonday replaced the crisp, frosty nip of the morning air gave certain promise of the approach of spring.

MOUTH OF THE SIND VALLEY

Again, when at length Srinagar, the capital of Kashmir, was reached, and I was back in my much-loved garden, still other signs of spring's arrival were evident. Violets, pansies, wallflowers, narcissus, crocuses, and daisies were out. A few green blades were showing through the brown grass. Rose leaf-buds were bursting. In one garden near a few apricot blossoms had actually bloomed. And the whole garden was filled with the spring song of the birds lightly turning to thoughts of love—thrushes, minas, sparrows, blue-tits, hoopoes, starlings; bold, familiar crows, and, most delightful of them all, the charming little bulbuls with their coquettish top-knots—the friendly little beings who come confidingly in at the windows and perch on the curtain rails or chairs, and even on the table to peck sugar from the basin.

And so for many days the weather continued, the temperature a degree or two below freezing-point 8at night, and rising to a maximum of 55° in the shade and 105° in the sun in the day-time. Day after day cloudlessly clear. The snowy ranges standing out sharp and distinct. The nearer mountains still covered with snow to within a thousand or two feet of the valley level. In the early morning all the valley-bottom glistening silvery-white with hoar frost. Then towards noon a curious struggle between summer and winter. The aspect of the country outside the garden entirely winter—leafless trees and frost-withered grass; but in the still air the sun's rays, with daily increasing power, having all the warmth of an early summer day in England; and under the noonday sun the mountains fading in a dreamy haze.

Then, of a sudden, came one of those complete and rapid changes which so enhance the charm of Kashmir. Dark ominous clouds settled on the near mountain-tops; here and there sweeping along their summits whirling snowstorms were driven along; the distant snows showed up with that steel-grey definition which in storm-ridden days replaces the dreamy indistinctness of more sunny times; now and then a glinting sun-ray breaking through the driving clouds would brighten up 9some solitary peak; and in the valley bottom periods of threatening stillness would alternate with gusty bursts of wind.

SUNSET ON THE WULAR LAKE

Such signs are usually the presage of unpleasant weather. But in the present case rain did not fall; and this was fortunate, for I had gone into camp to shoot a bara-singh, the famous Kashmir stag. Rising at four on the following morning, and, as soon as I had had a hurried breakfast, mounting a shaggy, naughty little pony captured in the fighting in Tibet, I followed the shadowy form of a shikari bestriding a still more diminutive country pony. Most of the clouds of the previous day had disappeared. The wind had died down, and the stars were shining out with that clear brilliance only seen amidst the mountains and in the desert. There was a sharp, bracing feeling in the air—not the same stinging cold I had felt when riding along this road at night in January, but strong and invigorating. We stumbled along on our ponies across fields and by paths which only a native could detect. At each village dogs howled dismally at us, but not a soul was astir. We gradually approached the dark outlines of the mountains, and near their base, while it was still pitch dark, we were joined by other shikaris who, like stage conspirators and with bated breath, explained where a stag had been seen on the previous day. I had then to dismount and walk; steadily and silently we ascended the mountain-side, and by sunrise were 3000 feet above the valley. The shikaris were now visible, and like their class hard and keen-looking, clearly used to living on mountain-sides in cold and heat, and to be ever peering into distances. The head shikari was a grey, grizzled, old-looking man, though I daresay he was really not over fifty; hard and tough, and very grave and earnest—for to him all else in the world is play, and shikar is man's real work in life. Residents, no doubt, have some employments to amuse themselves with in ordinary times; but when the real business of life has to be done they come to him, and he takes them gently in hand like little children, and shows them the haunts of the Kashmir stag, his habits, where he wanders, and how to pursue him.

DAWN IN THE NULLA

So now I put myself humbly in charge of the shikaris, for I make no pretence to be a sportsman. They thereupon proceed to whisper together with profound earnestness and dramatic action. They point out the exact spot where, on the previous afternoon, a stag was seen. They pick up little tufts of his hair brushed off, as they say, in fighting. They show his footsteps in the soft soil and on patches of snow. And they are full of marvellous conjectures as to where he can have gone. But gone he has, and that was the main fact which no amount of whispering could get over.

So on we went along the mountain-side, and now through deep snow, for we were on a northward-facing slope of an outlying spur—and all slopes which face northward are wooded, while southward-facing slopes are bare. The explanation was evident. For on the latter slopes the sun's rays fell directly and almost at right angles, and in consequence fallen snow quickly disappears: while on the northern slopes the sun's rays only slant across the surface; the snow remains much longer; the moisture in the soil is retained; vegetation flourishes; trees grow up; they in their turn still further shade the snow, and with their roots retain the moisture. And so as a net result one side of a mountain is clothed in dense forest, and on the other there may not be a single tree. Thus it is that on the southern side of Kashmir, that is, on the *northward*-facing slopes of the Pir Panjal range, there is, as at Gulmarg, dense and continuous forest, while on the northern side of the valley, on the slope of the hill that consequently faces southward, there is no forest except on the slopes of those subsidiary spurs which face northward.

We followed the tracks of the stag through this patch of forest, mostly of hazels, the shikaris pointing out where the stag had nibbled off the young leaf-buds and bark which seem to form the staple food of the deer at this time of year. At last we came to another shikari who said he had seen the stag that very morning. But I suspect this was merely a form of politeness to reinspire my lagging hope, for though I went down and up and along the mountain-side, and spent the whole day there, I saw no stag. Once we heard a rustling among the leaves, and hope revived, but it was merely a troop of monkeys. A little later a boar shuffled out; and again, on a distant spur, disporting himself in the sunshine, we saw a bear; but no stag.

KOTWAL FROM THE FOREST ABOVE KANGAN, SIND VALLEY

Still, in spite of the exertion and in spite of the disappointment, a day like this on the mountain-side is felt as one of the days in which one lives. The air was fresh and bracing. There was something both soothing and inspiring in the quiet of the mountains and the immense distances before me. Far away to the south majestic clouds and snowstorms were sweeping along the snowy range of the Pir Panjal. Beneath was the placid river wending its tortuous way through the peaceful valley. On one hand would be seen angry storm-clouds rolling threateningly across with numerous sun-rays piercing through and lighting up the serpentine course of the river. On the other, emerging from the black masses, would appear the sunlit snowy range, not hard, defined, and clear, and rooted on earth, but to all appearances hung from the heavens like an ethereal transparency.

Hour after hour I alternately feasted on the changing scenes displayed across the valley, and with my field-glasses searched the mountain-side for bara-singh. When evening closed in I returned to camp, where business kept me on the following day, but on the day after I again rode out while it was yet dark. As the first faint signs of dawn appeared I began the ascent of the mountain with the shikaris. The heavens were clear and cloudless. The bluey-black of the sky imperceptibly faded into grey. The mountain slowly turned from grey to brown as we steadily worked upward. The reposeful stillness which is the characteristic charm 14of the mountains was only broken by the cheerful chuckle of the chikor, or the occasional twitter of a bird calling to its mate. Then as we reached the summit of a ridge, and I looked out through the greys and browns, a sudden thrill struck through me as, all unexpectedly, my eye lit on the long flush of rosy pink which the yet unrisen sun had thrown upon the distant mountains, and which was the more pronounced and striking because their skyey background and their base was still the grey of night. Not often does one see a range of *rosy* mountains. And even now the effect lasted for a short time only. For rapidly a faint blue drowned the grey. The sky grew bluer and bluer. The valley became filled with light. But, alas! the rosy pink that had flushed the snowy summits faded imperceptibly away to barren whiteness. The whole long range of mountains showed themselves out with admirable clearness, but distinctly rooted in the unromantic brown of the valley.

ABOVE THE CAMPING-GROUND, SONAMARG, SIND VALLEY

By seven we were at the summit of the mountain with the sun now shining full upon us, the air crisp and frosty-the very ideal of young and vigorous day. We marched steadily along the ridge searching the hollows on either side for stag, but all we saw was a boar breaking the ice in a 15pool on the ridge to get a morning drink. At length we halted for refreshment and rest still on the summit of the ridge with the most beautiful valley on earth spread out in all its loveliness 3000 feet below, and the heavenly snowy range bounding the horizon from end to end before us. Just faintly the sounds from some village below would be wafted to us through the clear still air. But otherwise we seemed serenely apart from the noisy turmoil of humanity; and bathed in the warm noonday sunlight I was able to drink in all the spirit of the loveliness around me.

And there came upon me this thought, which doubtless has occurred to many another besides myself—why the scene should so influence me and yet make no impression on the men about me. Here were men with far keener eyesight than my own, and around me were animals with eyesight keener still. Their eyes looked on the same scene as mine did, and could distinguish each detail with even greater accuracy. Yet while I lay entranced with its exquisite beauty the keen-eyed shikaris, the animals, and the soaring eagle above me, might have been stone blind for all the impression of beauty it left upon them. Clearly it is not the eye, but the soul that sees. But then comes the still 16further reflection—what may there not be staring *me* straight in the face which I am as blind to as the Kashmir stags are to the beauties amidst which they spend their entire lives? The whole panorama may be vibrating with beauties man has not yet the soul to see. Some already living, no doubt, see beauties that we ordinary men cannot appreciate. It is only a century ago that mountains were looked upon as hideous. And in the long centuries to come may we not develop a soul for beauties unthought of now? Undoubtedly we must. And often in reverie on the mountains I have tried to imagine what still further loveliness they may yet possess for men.

From clambering over the high mountains in search of a solitary stag to sitting in a boat in the middle of a lake with thousands of ducks incessantly swishing round, is only one other example of the variety of scene and interest which Kashmir affords. There was just time before the end of the season for a final duck shoot, and eight of us rode or drove out six miles from Srinagar to the famous Hokrar Ghat, "jheel," which the Maharaja had so kindly placed at the disposal of the Resident for the season.17

THE KAJNAG FROM SOPUR, EARLY SPRING

We meet at the edge of the lake and draw lots for the numbered butts. The shikaris, boatmen, and boats are awaiting us, and as soon as we have decided where each is to go, and have fixed a time to cease shooting as an interval for lunch, and to give the ducks time to settle again for the further shooting in the afternoon, we embark each on a light shallow skiff with our guns, cartridges, and tiffin, and glide out through a narrow channel in the reeds to the open water beyond.

Hokrar is right in the centre of the valley, and from the lake a complete elliptical ring of snowy mountains can be seen. The nearest and most conspicuous peak is Haramokh, 16,903 feet, and 24 miles distant. From this the eye ranges from peak to peak to the Khagan range 70 miles distant in the extreme west of the valley; then along over the Kaj Nag mountains separated by the gorge of the Jhelum River valley from the Pir Panjal range, which forms the southern boundary of the valley with Gulmarg, 24 miles distant, on its southern slopes. Then traversing the whole length of the Pir Panjal range from the highest point, Tatakute, 15,524 feet, the eye falls to the depression over which lies the Banihal 18Pass, and rising again meets the Kishtwar range 65 miles distant, closing in the valley on the east, from whence the eye wanders on snowy ranges till Haramokh in the north again is met.

The day was another of glorious sunshine, and in the noonday sun the southern range was bathed in dazzling light, the northern showed up sharp and clear with the sun's rays beating straight upon it, while the distant ranges right and left faded away in haze and dreamland. Soft woolly clouds floated along the mountain-sides. A sharp, crisp air freshened one up and broke the water into dancing glittering ripples on which innumerable duck were bobbing up and down.

Here we shot for a couple of hours before tiffin, and afterwards till evening closed in. It was not one of the great shoots like we have in the autumn, and which I will describe later, but was none the less enjoyable, and being the last of the season each made the most of it.

KOTWAL FROM NEAR THE DAL DARWAZA

At the end of March I visited Harwan, a very favourite spot, once the abode of a famous Buddhist saint, and now best known as the site of the reservoir for the water-supply of Srinagar and of the tanks for trout-breeding. Rain had 19fallen in the night, and heavy clouds hung overhead with only occasional glimpses of intensely clear blue sky between them. But spring was now clearly advancing. The great chenar trees, two and three centuries old, were still bare, but the willows were showing fresh young leaves; the apricot trees were covered with clouds of blossom, pink and white. The mountain-sides were dotted with white wild cherry and pear and apple in full bloom; the ground was often white like snow with the fallen petals; the young hazel-nut leaves gave freshness to the mountain-side; and near at hand were violets, anemones, and cuckoo flowers. The air was rich with the scent of the fruit trees. Swarms of bees were humming around them; butterflies—tortoise-shell, clouded yellow, and cabbage-white—fluttered in the sunshine; and the lively twittering of birds—bulbuls, goldfinches, wagtails, and tits—gave yet one further evidence of the awakening spring.

Each spot in Kashmir one is inclined to think the most beautiful of all—perhaps because each in some particular excels the rest. Certainly Harwan has many fascinations of its own. Rising sheer behind was a mountain crowned with dark precipices overhung by heavy clouds through which 20pierced the snowy summit. Clear crystal streams rushed along the valley with a cheery rustling sound. In the middle distance lay the placid Dal Lake—on the far side overshadowed by the Hari Parbat fort. The main valley was interspersed with village clumps of fresh willow, clouds of fruit blossom, and majestic chenars. In the far distance lay the snowy ranges of the Pir Panjal, the Kaj Nag, and Khagan; and facing round again to the north rose the striking Mahadeo peak—rocky, bold and precipitous, and pine-clad to near the summit.

And one of the further attractions of Kashmir is not only that each spot is so different from the other, but that each spot has a different aspect every day. Bright days are the more numerous, but dull days also have no less striking attractions. The day after our arrival at Harwan was still and heavy; the whole sky was overhung with clouds, though they were high above the mountains, and even the most distant ranges showed up with unusual clearness white and distinct against the grey monotone sky. The stillness and the heavy cloud evidently portended a storm, and in the afternoon the distant horizon grew darker and darker. The snowy mountains were gradually 21obscured from view. Then the middle distance became black and threatening. At the same time on the mountain craigs behind heavy clouds imperceptibly settled down, and the great cliff grew darker and darker. Blackness seemed to grow all round, and the mountain summits with the angry clouds upon them looked more and more sombre and threatening. Meanwhile all was still and noiseless. Then suddenly out of the stillness came a rush of air. The poplar trees bent like whips. The long shoots of the willow trees lashed backwards and forwards. Great drops of rain came spitting down. A bright, quick flash darted out from the mountain. Then crash came the thunder—clap after clap—and torrents of rain. Few things in Nature are more impressive than a thunderstorm among the mountains.

THE LULL BEFORE THE STORM, DAL LAKE

When next I visited Harwan in the middle of May spring had given way to early summer. The mountain-sides were dotted over with clumps of yellow barberry and wild pink roses; clematis was in bloom, and honeysuckle was trailing from the trees. On the ground were large wild geraniums, the big purple iris, white dead nettle, yellow potentillas, strawberry blossom, tom-thumbs, 22clover, ferns, speedwell, and primulas. The rocks by the stream were often covered with ivy and overhung by sprays of pink roses. While on the mountain-sides, on the northward-facing slopes, the wild apricot, cherry, and wych hazel, and in the valley bottom willow, mulberry, and walnut were in full leaf. And among the birds were now golden orioles, wagtails (white and yellow), kingfishers, herons, water-robins, buntings, grey tits, wren warblers, paradise fly-catchers, bulbuls, thrushes, redstarts, pigeons, doves, and shrikes.

The morning was cloudy and misty, but again with special beauties of its own. Long streaks of mist were drifting along the mountain-sides, all at precisely the same level. Mahadeo, 15,000 feet, was at first quite clear and lighted by the sun. Then a mist drifted towards it, and rapidly, but by almost imperceptible increase, the cloud enveloped it. Light misty clouds swirled about the mountain as currents and counter-currents seized them. Anon the mist in great part cleared away, and Mahadeo was seen peering through the clouds, bold and supernaturally high. Then the peak and all the mountain-sides were enveloped in dark heavy clouds, rain fell, and there seemed every prospect of a wet and gloomy day. But all unexpectedly 23rifts again appeared, and Mahadeo was once more seen rising composedly above the clouds, the young green foliage standing out distinct and bright, and each rock sharp and well defined. And so, hour after hour, the struggle between cloud and sunshine, between good and evil continued, it being impossible to tell at any moment which was more likely to prevail. The clouds seemed settling down, then a glint of sunshine was seen high on some upland lighting the fresh green grass and some stray shepherd hut. Finally wet prevailed, and the mist settled lower and lower on the valley, the rain poured down and a seemingly regular rainy day set in. But there was fascination yet in watching the mists floating along the mountains, forming and dispersing, enshrouding and revealing the mountain peaks; and the green of the little valley showed up greener than ever. The mountain-sides, usually so brown, were seen to be tinged with a delicate shade of green. The poplars, mulberries, and chenars at the mouth of the valley had each their own especial tint. The rice-fields showed up in brilliant emerald.

ABOVE LIDARWAT, LIDAR VALLEY

Yet after it had appeared to settle down for a whole day's rain the mists suddenly cleared away from the mountain. The sun broke through the 24clouds and showed up the rounded higher spurs with the soft, downy brown of an Oriental carpet, and the higher peaks stood out sharp and clear. An hour later long level lines of mist appeared and swiftly grew thicker, the whole mountain from one level upward was once more enveloped in cloud which thus gained the final victory.

Harwan village itself at this time of year was strikingly picturesque. It was enshrouded in massive clumps of chenar foliage, below which were the lighter shades of the willow, mulberry, and walnut, and the straight, graceful, white-trunked poplars piercing through. Here and there a horse-chestnut in full flower lit up the foliage, and most beautiful of all were the patches of tall irises—dark purple, mauve, and white—which now surrounded the village. Numerous water-courses rushing through the village lands gave brightness, cheeriness, and a sense of coolness; while the crowing of cocks, the twittering of the birds, the lowing of cattle, and the neighing of the ponies grazing on the rich green grass in the valley bottom, and the distant calls of the shepherd boy to the flocks of sheep and goats on the mountain, gave further animation to the scene. And whether it 25was more entrancing now, or three weeks later when the irises were over, but when it was wreathed in white roses, it would be difficult to say. Irises and roses are the two especial beauties of Kashmir villages and Kashmir lanes and hedgerows. And I would not like to positively state which was the more beautiful—the rich clumps of mauve and purple irises surrounding the village with warmth and colour in the spring, or the clustering wreaths of roses, white and pink, brightening the village lands and hedgerows in the summer.

SUNSET ON THE JHELUM, ABOVE SRINAGAR

Only one desire we must feel in regard to these villages—that all this natural beauty could not be further enhanced by the trim little cottages of rural England or the picturesque chalets of Switzerland. Every time one sees a Kashmir village and succumbs to the charm of all that Nature has done for it, one longs to see the squalor, untidiness, and dirt of house and man and clothing removed, and justice done by man to what Nature has done for *him*.

Harwan is not only noted for its natural beauty, and as having been the abode of a celebrated Buddhist saint: it is also now remarkable as possessing a hatchery of English trout, the ordinary brown trout, and of Danube trout or huchon; 26and here can be seen English trout of all sizes up to 11 lbs.

These trout were first placed in the Dachigam stream which runs through the valley opening out at Harwan; and now all up this valley ideal trout-fishing is given by H.H. the

Maharaja to his guests. And what more perfect spot for the purpose could be found? Kept as a close preserve for two purposes; firstly, for stag-shooting; and, secondly, to insure the freshness of the water which furnishes the water-supply of the whole city of Srinagar, it is absolutely quiet and peaceful. There are no inhabitants, and no life but wild life; and, except for the superior grandeur of the mountains on either side, it exactly resembles a Highland valley. We see the same clear rushing river, here dashing over boulders in a series of rapids, and there lying in cool, peaceful pools alongside a grassy bank or beneath some overshadowing trees. On a cloudy day, when the high mountains are shrouded in mist and a gentle rain is falling, you might be in Scotland itself. On a fine day, with Mahadeo towering 10,000 feet immediately above you, and with glimpses of snowy ranges in the distance, you have Scotland and something *more*.

SPRING IN KASHMIR

This is the valley especially reserved for the 27sport of Viceroys, and here it was that in the autumn of 1906 the Maharaja entertained Lord Minto. And well do I remember the intense relief of the Viceroy as he turned into the valley and left all ceremonials and State business behind, and felt that here at least he was in a haven of rest and natural enjoyment. The air was clear and bracing, the sky cloudless, and the evening sun throwing long soothing shadows up the valley. Who could feel a care while he fished or hunted stag in a valley with more than the beauty and with all the freshness of his native land?

I have said so much about Harwan and the Dachigam valley as they are typical of the prettiest parts of rural Kashmir and the side-valleys, but I must now return to the description of Srinagar and the main valley itself and go back to where we left it in the spring. On April 1st, the chief glory of the Kashmir spring, peach trees were in full blossom, and forming in the landscape little clouds of the purest and most delicate pink, and giving it an exquisite touch of light and colour. The taller and larger pear trees were snow-white masses. The pink-tinged apple blossoms, the chenar, and walnut leaves were just appearing, and the poplar 28and mulberry leaves showed faint symptoms of bursting. We were in the first, most delicate flush of early youthful spring.

A mile from Srinagar, on the way to Gupkar and the Dal Lake, the road passes over a gap between the Takht-i-Suliman and the range to the north. This spot is well known as "The Gap"; and as it is perhaps a hundred feet above the valley level an extensive view is obtained, on the one hand, over the great vale of Kashmir to the snowy Pir Panjal range in the background on the south, and on the other hand to the Dal Lake, Haramokh, and the mountain range, close by on the north. There were very few days when either in the morning or evening I did not visit this spot, and hardly ever did I see the same view. Every day there seemed some fresh beauty; and which day in spring, and whether the days in spring were more beautiful than the days in autumn, I could never satisfy myself. On April 1st, looking southward, there was first on the sloping foreground an almond orchard with a sprinkling of trees in white and pink blossom and the remainder in young leaf. Then in the valley bottom were clumps of willows in the freshest yellowy green; light green wheat-fields; bunches of chenar trees 29not yet in leaf; broad reaches of the placid river glistening in the sunshine, with numerous boats gliding gracefully on its surface; and away over the valley were little clusters of villages, with the land gradually rising to that range of snowy mountains which forms the culminating touch of beauty in every Kashmir scene.

ON THE DAL LAKE IN SPRING

Looking in the opposite direction from the Gap towards the Dal Lake was a less extensive, but scarcely less attractive scene. On the foreground of the gentle slopes towards the lake were tall pear trees in fresh white bloom dotted prettily among the fields of new green wheat. Away to the left was an orchard of peach in the purest and lightest of pink. Little hamlets nestled among the fruit trees; and immediately beyond them stretched the still, clear lake reflecting in its mirror surface the graceful willows and chenar trees by its edge, and the mountain ranges by which it was encircled. As it seemed floating in its midst lay the famous Isle of Chenars mirrored again in its glassy surface. By its shore stretched the renowned Moghal gardens—the Nishat Bagh and the Shalimar Bagh—with their grand avenues of chenars sloping to the water's edge. Above the far border rose a mountain ridge still clothed in snow; above that again the lofty 30Haramokh; and away in the extreme distance lay the fairy Khagan snows, while on the whole scene there swam a purple-bluey haze, growing more purple and more blue the more distant it fell, and giving to all a softening sense of peace and ease. For tenderness of restful beauty this scene is not excelled.

So far the weather had been exceptionally fine and warm for the season, and the rainfall to date from the commencement of the year had been three inches below the normal; but now a wet spell set in such as one has to expect in the spring in Kashmir, which is always very

7

uncertain. On April 12th there were 2¾ inches of rain. The total for the year now exceeded the normal by four inches. The river rapidly rose ten feet, flooded all the low-lying fields, and seriously threatened the European quarter; and, finally, snow fell in Srinagar itself. The maximum temperature in the shade rose to only 50° while the minimum at night fell to 33°. It is always the exceptional which happens—in weather at any rate. So this must not be expected every year. But something else exceptional will occur whatever year we choose, and there is little use in describing a normal year, for no such year ever comes in real life.31

On the road into Kashmir very serious breaks were made by the rain and by the melting snow and the mud floods which it brought down. Whole stretches of road were completely carried away and wiped out of existence. Bridges were broken; and so dangerous were the falling boulders, that one European was knocked straight into the Jhelum River and drowned, and several natives were badly injured. The dak bungalows were crammed with travellers rolling up from behind, and we subsequently heard of the misery they suffered from overcrowded rooms, from the never-ending rolling of the thunder, and the incessant pelting of the rain. The beauties of Kashmir cannot be attained without suffering, and the suffering on the road up is often considerable.

A hard-worked member of the Government of India came from Calcutta to spend a ten-days' holiday with us in the middle of this deluge, and as day after day of his holiday went by with nothing but rain, our pride in the glories of Kashmir sank lower and lower, and we feared he would go back to give the country but an evil reputation. But the final day of his stay redeemed all, and for that single day he was good enough to say he would have come the whole way from Calcutta. We drove 32out along the shores of the Dal Lake to the Nishat Bagh, and anything more exquisitely lovely than the combination of the freshness of the young spring green, with the whiteness of the snow now low down on the mountain-sides with the blue sky, the brilliant sunshine, the dreamy purply haze, the mirror lake, the yellow mustard fields, and the clouds of pink and white fruit blossom now in its perfection, this earth can surely nowhere show.

The lake was full from the recent rain, and lapped up to the edge of the garden. On either side of the gateway were masses of Kashmir lilac. Stretching up the mountain-side, on either side of the line of fountains and waterfalls which flowed down from the upper end of the garden, was a long avenue of massive chenar trees just freshly tinted with budding foliage, and at the sides and by the entrance were peach, and pear, and cherry in brilliant bloom. Slowly we ascended the avenue, and then from the top looked down between the great chenar trees, over the cascades falling to the lake, over the smooth green turf, over the clumps of purple iris, over the white cherry blossom and the mauve lilac; to the still waters of the lake; to the willows and poplars along its edge; to the fort of Hari Parbat; and then on to 33the radiant snows now glistening more brightly, and looking more ethereal and lovely than ever before. Spring is beautiful everywhere. Spring is more beautiful in Kashmir than anywhere else, and in a Kashmir spring this was the most beautiful day of all.

ENTRANCE TO THE MAR CANAL

Yet another attractive spot near Srinagar is the site of the original city founded by Asoka at Pandrathan, three miles distant on the Islamabad road. Here at the end of a spur running down from the mountains and jutting out to meet a bend in the river, stands the remains of an immense monolith lingam on the levelled edge of the spur, eighty feet or so above the river. Immediately beneath is a majestic bend of the river, and one April evening when I visited the sight I looked out from the raised plateau up two glistening reaches, bordered by fresh green grass and overhung by graceful willows and poplars in their newest foliage. The wheat-fields on the opposite bank were a brilliant emerald, and the fields of glowing yellow mustard and young linseed interspersed with scarlet poppies gave a relieving touch of colour. All the valley was dotted over with picturesque hamlets half-hidden in clumps of 34willow and over-towering chenar trees. The recent floods gave a lake-like appearance to the middle distance. On the right the temple on the Takht-i-Suliman formed a graceful feature in the scene; and from there completely round the semicircle to the distant left stretched the dreamy snowy mountains, hazy immediately under the sun, but white and distinct when the evening sun struck full upon them. A more fitting site for worship could hardly be found.

In full summer the Kashmir valley is, perhaps, in its least interesting condition. The snow has nearly melted from the mountains. They are often hidden by heat-haze or dust. The fruit blossoms are all over. The yellow mustard and the blue linseed in the fields have gone to seed. The green of the trees has lost its freshness; and the prevailing tones are heavy greens and browns. The weather too is sultry. The thermometer rises to 95° or 97° in the shade. A heavy, lethargic feeling oppresses one. Mosquitoes appear in swarms. And by the end of June every one who can flees to Gulmarg, to Pahlgam in the Lidar valley, to Sonamarg in the Sind, to Gurais and to the numerous other cool mountain resorts.

THE TEMPLE, CHENAR BAGH

But early in September the valley renews its charms and visitors return. The atmosphere has been freshened and cooled by the rains which, though they fall lightly in the valley itself, are often heavy on the surrounding mountains. The ripe rice-fields show an expanse of green and yellow often two or three miles in extent. The villages, dirty and untidy at close quarters, it is true, but nestling among the chenars, willows, poplars, walnuts, and mulberries, show as entrancing islands amidst the sea of rice. Ponies browse among the marshes up to their knees in water; and groups of cattle graze along the grassy edge of the streams and water-ducts.

The sun is still powerful in the daytime, and the sky usually bright and clear. But the monsoon will often make a few final efforts. One such day I note when voluminous masses of cloud rolled up from behind the Pir Panjal to a height of twenty-five or thirty thousand feet, their westward edges aglow from the setting sun, and showing clear and distinct against the background of pinky light blue sky, while the great main volume remained dark, heavy, and sombre, with now and then a spit of lightning flashing out, and on the far side, away from the setting sun, threatening tentacles stretched out across the valley in unavailing effort to reach the mountains on the northern side. Under these mighty monsoon masses even the great mountains looked dwarfed and puny. It was a great and final effort of that stupendous natural phenomenon which bears the waters of the Indian Ocean to beat upon the Himalaya; and as an omen that the monsoon was now over, the sky behind the storm-clouds was intensely clear and tranquil, and the moon slowly ascended in undisturbed serenity.

And the rainy season being finished there now commenced almost the most charming time of all, not, indeed, with the freshness of spring, but with more certainty of continual brightness and light, and more vigour and strength in the air, and above all, with that warmth and richness of colour in the foliage which makes an autumn in Kashmir unique. Towards the end of October the green of the immense masses of chenar slowly turns to purple, red, and yellow, and every intervening shade. The poplars, mulberries, and apricots add each their quota of autumnal beauty. The valley and the river edge are resplendent in the gorgeous colouring. And beautiful as is the spring, I was tempted to think that even more exquisitely lovely still was the bright autumnal day when we drifted down the river in our house-boat, when all the chenars along the river bank were loaded with the richest and most varied colouring, when the first fresh fall of snow on the mountains was glistening in the radiant sunshine, and there ran through the air that restful sense of certainty that this was no hurried pleasure snatched from a stormy season, but that for day after day and week after week one might count on the same brilliant sunshine, the same clear, blue sky, and daily increasing crispness, freshness, and vigour in the air.

RUINS OF LALLA ROOKH'S GARDENS, LAKE MANASBAL

The great broad reaches in the river, glistening in the sunlight and fringed with the rich autumnal foliage, were superlatively beautiful. Shadipur, at the junction of the Sind River, where there is a little temple on an island and hoary old chenars drooping over it to the water's surface, was a dream of all that is most lovely. And the Manasbal Lake, so fresh and deep and clear, set like a jewel among the mountains, with clumps and avenues of these same red and purple foliaged trees upon its edge, and reflecting in its surface the white snowy range of the distant Pir Panjal, was the supreme gem of all Kashmir. All these are beauties which one cannot describe, for whatever one may say, the reality must ever remain more beautiful than the picture. But perhaps by the unison of pen and brush some faint impression of the loveliness of a Kashmir autumn may yet have been conveyed.

This season to the sportsman also is the most enjoyable. For now come in the duck and geese from far-away Siberia, halting here for a time in the lakes and marshes on their way to India. I have already described a duck-shoot in spring. In the autumn there is still finer shooting, for the duck have come in fresh and are in greater numbers than on their return journey. As I have already said, the Maharaja most hospitably places at the disposal of the Resident the shooting on the Hokrar Lake and marsh, which affords some of the best duck-shooting in the world, and it was here that Lord Minto and party shot over 1500 duck in one day in 1906.

Last year we had our first shoot on October 4th. We rode for six miles in the fresh morning air and brilliant sunshine to the edge of the lake, where the shikaris and boatmen were awaiting us. Over the reeds and over the open expanse of water beyond there was that glorious view of the distantly encircling mountains which I have before described. The lower slopes were at this season a reddish pink which merged into the rich purply blue of the higher and more distant portion of the range. Soft fleecy clouds and a hazy blue in the sky gave a dreamy tone to the scene. Many kinds of waterfowl were lazily disporting themselves on the water and among the reeds. The surface was often covered with numerous flat, round leaves and pure white waxy water-lilies with rich yellow centres.

Through these we were paddled swiftly to the butts, which were skilfully hidden among the reeds, and here amid clouds of mosquitoes, dragon-flies, and gnats, we awaited the first shot to be fired by the occupant of the farthest butt. The sun beat powerfully down. All was still, and drowsy, and silent, save for the drone of the flies and the occasional "quack, quack!" of the ducks paddling unsuspiciously on the lake.

At last a distant shot was heard, and then a suppressed roar, as of breakers on a far-off shore. Then from the direction of the shot a black cloud arose and advanced rapidly upon us. The roar increased, and in a few seconds the whole sky was covered with a whirling, swishing, whizzing flight of ducks. Thousands and thousands of them: flashing past from right to left, from left to right, backwards and forwards, forwards and backwards, 40in bewildering multitudes. For the moment one's breath was absolutely taken away. There was such a swish and swirl it was impossible to aim. Then as the first wild rush was over it became easier to be deliberate, and duck after duck fell to my companions' guns.

After a quarter of an hour or so a lull occurred. In the distance, flights of duck were seen circling high in the air, but none came near. A lazy interval ensued. The sun beat down with unexpected force. Perspiration poured down head and neck. Dragon-flies, blue and red, large and small, with gauze-like wings and brilliant bodies, floated swiftly but noiselessly among the reeds. The purring of the crickets, the occasional twitter of birds, the swishing of high flights of duck far out of reach, the call of a goose and the bang of a distant gun at intervals broke the silence; but otherwise all was wrapped in dreamy noonday stillness. Then, of a sudden, another succession of flights of duck came whizzing past, and as fast as we could fire the gun was put to the shoulder. Another lull followed, only to be succeeded by more flights, and so on through the day. At 1.30, by previous arrangement, we stopped for lunch and to give the duck an opportunity of settling, then 41renewed the shooting till nightfall. At the end of the day Colonel Edwards, the Residency Surgeon, had himself shot 203, and others had shot well over the hundred.

From this time onward, on three or four days in each month, the duck-shooting on this famous lake continues. The weather now gets gradually colder, till by December there are sixteen degrees of frost. All the leaves have now left the trees. The grass is quite brown. But the days are nearly always fine and clear; and though there will be thick ice and long icicles in the early morning, by ten or eleven all the ice not in the shade has disappeared, the air is pleasantly warm, and there is seldom any wind.

Christmas brings a round of festivities, dances, dinners, and children's parties, for even in the winter as many as seventy or eighty will assemble at a dance, and occasional outside travellers or sportsmen drop in all through the winter. After Christmas a change in weather sets in. Clouds bank up and snow or rain falls. January and February are the worst months in the year.

But just before leaving the valley this last year I had one further attempt to shoot a Kashmir stag. Six miles out from Srinagar, up the valley, 42we had a little camp on the edge of the river—a lovely spot in summer when the rich foliage overhangs the water, and when the grassy banks are green and fresh, and the river is full up to the lip; but now when the trees were bare, the banks brown and bleak, and the water at its lowest, an uninviting-looking spot. Moreover, the sky was overcast and threatening. Women who came to draw water from the river were pale and shivering. Our servants were huddled up with the cold. A raw wind whistled down the valley, and snow threatened on the higher mountain.

This latter was precisely what I wanted, for it would drive the stag down to the lower ridges when I would be stalking next day. At four in the morning, therefore, I rose, and after a solid early breakfast mounted my faithful but naughty Tibetan pony, and, accompanied by a guide, rode for seven miles through the darkness and frosty but invigorating air to the foot of the hills, where the two shikaris awaited me.

Like their class, they were hard, keen-looking men, accustomed to live on the mountain-side, to weather hardship and exposure, and live with Nature and wild animals—an altogether different type from the crafty townsman or indolent dwellers on boats. 43Rahem Sheikh, the chief, was a grizzled old man, with keen, far-seeing eyes, tough physique, and a grave, earnest demeanour as if the business of his life was of the most serious. This, indeed, as I have already said, is a special trait of head shikaris all India over; and during viceregal visits to Native States I have never been able to decide which takes himself most seriously—the head shikari or the European caterer. Both look upon the Viceroy, the Chief, and the Resident, in the way of children who are to be indulged. They have to be amused and fed. They no doubt have unimportant business of their own. But the really serious business in this life is—to the shikari to find game, and to the caterer to provide food. Things would rub along somehow or other without a Viceroy; but how would life be without the head shikari to show the stag, or the caterer to produce meat and drink?

Knowing the point of view of head shikaris I placed myself, therefore, with child-like but misplaced confidence in his hand. But, alas! snow had not fallen on the higher mountains. The clouds had cleared away, and the stags must have remained on the distant peaks—many miles away and thousands of feet higher. Two days 44of hard climbing and careful search produced no result.

On the third day, rising early and looking out of my tent, I saw a perfectly clear sky and the ground covered thick with hoar frost; a sharp crisp nip was in the air, the thermometer registered 16° Fahr., and away across the glistening reach in the river appeared a rose-pink range of mountains showing up sharply against the clear blue sky. Let the reader imagine a frosty morning in the Thames valley. Let him imagine, what we never have in England, a really clear blue sky. And then, filling up the distant end of one of its most beautiful reaches, let him imagine a lofty range of rose-coloured mountains; and he will then have a picture of the view from my camp at sunrise on the January morning.

Mounting my pony, I rode off in the now radiant sunshine to another hill-side nine miles distant. The frosty morning air at first nipped my ears and fingers, but the hard galloping soon sent the blood tingling through my veins, and in little over an hour I again joined the shikaris. With bated breath and significant glances at the mountain-side, they informed me that they had seen seven hinds and two stags, though the latter were both small.45

I dismounted, and left the wicked little Tibetan with his head well buried in a bundle of grass; and then with a coolie to carry my tiffin, overcoat, and rifle, started up the hill-side. One quickly becomes fit in such a climate. This was my third day out, and now I climbed the mountain almost as easily as the shikaris themselves. What on the first day was a decided effort was now a scarcely perceptible strain. Perhaps, too, the greater expectation of finding a stag had something to do with the increased elasticity with which I ascended the mountain. Anyhow, taking off my coat, as with the exertion of climbing and in the brilliant sunshine it was now really hot, I was on the summit of the ridge 3000 feet above the valley, almost without noticing the climb.

At our feet on the opposite side lay a cosy little side-valley with villages nestling among the chenar and mulberry trees. Behind us lay the broad main valley with the great river gliding through it; and away in the distance the rugged Pir Panjal mountains were glistening in the noonday sun.

The scenery was perfect. But again no stags were seen. Till dark we scoured the mountain-side, but all we saw were the tracks of stags—or 46may be hinds—leading away to the higher mountains.

Then I had to hurry back to camp, and the next day to Srinagar, to prepare for a long journey down to Calcutta for the very dull object of giving evidence to a Royal Commission on Decentralisation.

The cycle of the seasons has been completed; and the aspect of the valley under the varying conditions of spring and summer, autumn and winter, has been depicted. In another chapter I will describe the means and methods of travel.47

CHAPTER II
TRAVEL IN KASHMIR

I have known Kashmir for twenty-one years, and ever since I have known it people have said it is getting spoilt. "It is not now what it used to be" is so often said. When the cart-road was being built every one said it would be spoilt. And now, when the construction of a railway is in contemplation, exactly the same remark is made. The impression conveyed is that the pleasures of travel in Kashmir are surely and steadily deteriorating. And this, no doubt, is true in certain aspects. Supplies are dearer. Coolies demand higher wages. The visitor disposed to solitude more frequently encounters his fellow Britisher. These are decided drawbacks, and the visitor who telegraphs to Danjhibhoy for a tonga, to Nedou's for a room in the hotel, and to Cockburn's for a house-boat, and has simply to pay his fare and his 48hotel bill, no doubt pines for the virgin time of Kashmir travel before the rattle of the tongas or the tooting of the motor car was heard in the valley.

Yet I doubt if all was bliss in those "good old days." Certainly Moorcroft, the first Englishman to visit Kashmir, had no very comfortable time, and must often in his turn have pined for a good hotel, a clean room, and a decent dinner—and, who knows, for a game of golf? Moorcroft visited Kashmir in 1823, and first had enormous difficulty in obtaining from Ranjit Singh, the ruler of the Punjab, to whom Kashmir was then subject, leave to come to Kashmir at all. He arrived there from the north in the autumn, and had fresh difficulty in obtaining permission to remain there for the winter. At the quarters he occupied he was "beset by crowds of people who not only filled the garden, but also came in boats." He was pursued wherever he went by inquisitive crowds, by importunate beggars, and by suspicious officials. When he wished to make short excursions from Srinagar objections were at once raised. When he was at length allowed to leave for the Lolab, officials were appointed to accompany him "to watch his proceedings and check inquisitiveness." 49 And when he finally left Kashmir for the Punjab by the Jhelum valley he was stopped by a small semi-independent chief near Uri, who demanded Rs. 15,000 as customs duty on his caravan, and as Moorcroft refused to pay more than Rs. 500 he was compelled to return to Srinagar and reach the Punjab by another route.

These certainly were not the halcyon days of Kashmir travel. But I suppose there must have been an intermediate time between then and now when travelling in Kashmir was perfection to those who had time enough at their disposal to "march" in. In those delightful times the traveller pitched his little camp wherever he wished. Grain was ridiculously cheap. Fowls were considered dear at twopence each. Coolies were thankful enough to get any payment at all. There were no game laws or game licences, so that the sportsman could shoot to his heart's content. The number of visitors for the year was restricted to 100, so that each had 700 or 800 square miles to himself, and there was no need of dress clothes, white shirts, or Ascot dresses.

When I first visited Kashmir in the autumn of 1887 its glory had already begun to depart, though as regards simplicity of travelling my methods 50 were of the simplest. I had no other clothes but what I stood in, and only the under portion of these were of European origin. All my outer clothes, including my boots, were worn out long before I reached Kashmir, and I was accordingly clothed in a long Central Asian robe and high native boots, for I was at the end of a journey of nearly four thousand miles from Peking. I had crossed—and was the first European to accomplish the feat—the Mustagh Pass, 19,000 feet high, into Baltistan; and the "Pass" being nothing else than a hard ice slope and a rocky precipice, down which I and my five servants and coolies had to let ourselves by means of turbans and waist-clothes tied together, I had been able to carry with me little even of the scanty baggage I had brought up to the other side of the Pass. I had indeed only a roll of bedding, which was thrown down the precipice, and a big kettle. I had no tent and no money! I had slept in the open from one side of the Himalayas to the other, and my funds were entirely exhausted, so that when I landed in Kashmir territory I had to borrow money from the Governor of Baltistan, Pandit Rada Kishen Kol, a very popular and respected official who is still in the Maharaja's service, and is now Chief Judge. 51

Simplicity of travel was, then, at least possible twenty years ago, and I managed, after crossing the Pass, to get along with only one servant who cooked, performed every function of the numerous servants we employ in India, and carried a load himself in emergency. But he was the most faithful, and my favourite of all the servants I have ever had. His name was Shukar Ali, and I must ask my reader's indulgence for a digression to describe him. I picked him up in Yarkand, in Chinese Turkestan, but he was a native of Ladak. He was the most cheery, happy-go-lucky, easy-going man, who ever proved a good servant in spite of his carelessness. Always laughing, always chaffing with the pony-men or coolies, always losing something vitally necessary, but always ready to do the hardest and most dangerous piece of work when the crucial moment arrived, he was the only Ladaki who dared to cross the Mustagh Pass with me, and but for one incident I would have a most grateful recollection of his services then. That incident I have often since reminded him of. After crossing the Pass we had to cross a very full and rapid stream flowing straight out of a glacier. Immense blocks of ice were breaking off the glacier and floating down 52 the stream. The bottom was also partly ice and partly boulder. Shukar Ali, with his usual readiness, volunteered to carry me across this stream on his back. But in mid-stream he slipped. I was precipitated into the icy water, while Shukar Ali, in his frantic efforts to regain his own footing, unknowingly kept pressing me under water. We both eventually gained the opposite bank all right. But I had no change of clothes, and every stitch I had on was wringing wet with ice-cold water.

When, two years later, Government sent me to explore all the northern frontier of Kashmir from Ladak and the Karakoram Pass to the Pamirs and Hunza, I again sought out Shukar Ali; and yet a third time, when I was sent on a political mission to Chinese Turkestan and the Pamirs in 1890-91. On each of these occasions he rendered unfailing service, and once both he and I were nearly drowned in an avalanche. We had been hewing our way up the steep slopes of an ice pass in a snowstorm, when suddenly out of the snow-clouds above us we heard a roar like thunder approaching nearer and nearer. We could not run if we would, for we were on an ice slope. We could only await our doom, for we knew it was an avalanche. But with a mighty rush it crashed 53 past a few paces in front of us, and we were safe.

A LADAKI IN SUMMER COSTUME

After 1891 I did not see Shukar Ali for seventeen years, for my travels never took me to that frontier again. But I heard of him from Dr. Sven Hedin who employed him in Tibet, and who told me of the wonderful tales which the imaginative Shukar Ali related of the journeys we had made together. And last summer the dear old man suddenly appeared at the Residency. He had heard that I was now Resident, and had walked 240 miles across the mountains to see me, and he presented himself wearing the identical coat I had given him seventeen years ago. He kept jumping up and down, first kissing my feet, then touching my coat, then salaaming, and all the time ejaculating an unceasing flow of speech, calling me by every affectionate term. Then from under numerous folds of his clothing he produced a wooden bowl, a bag full of sweets, a pair of goat horns for my wife and myself, and a marvellous collection of showy-looking stones which he had picked up in Tibet for my little girl.

He remained with me for a few weeks. I gave him something to keep him comfortable at home, but which I am sure in his good 54nature he will let his relations squeeze out of him, and then I sent him off back to Ladak. But before he left I asked the Maharaja to give him an order exempting him from service in his village. His Highness, with his usual kindness, readily acceded. An order was made out with the Maharaja's own signature attached, and at a garden-party at the Residency Shukar Ali was had up and presented with the order. His Highness addressed him in a most kindly manner, and on the following day presented him in Durbar with a shawl of honour.

Poor Shukar Ali left with many tearful farewell expressions, and a few weeks later I received from him the following letter:—

Sir—I reached very well home, with very felt happy and found all my poor family very well and showed the all kindly of your they got very glad, and we all family thankfully to you to remember us so much, to little people and my all friends got very glad too, they said thank you, and hope you would not be angry with this English written, please you pardon for this, and could not write myself and could not get other munshi write you, because and found Rassul, he was my old friend and let him write this letter. please give my salaam to Mem Sahib and Baby Baby Sahib.—Your obedient servantSHUKAR ALI

from poor Rassul plenty salaam,

the mark of Shukar Ali O.

55All this, however, is a digression, and I have to describe the normal modes of travel of the present day. Srinagar is 196 miles distant from the railway at Rawal Pindi, and is connected with it by a good cart-road—good, that is in its normal condition, but excessively bad after heavy rain, when at places the whole mountain-side slides down with the road into the river. The usual mode of conveyance is a tonga, a very common form of vehicle in the Indian "hills." It has two wheels, is drawn by a pair of ponies, has four seats back to back, and carries a mountain of luggage piled up on the splash-boards and on the roof. The ponies, when the season is not crowded and the road is good, gallop at full speed, and are changed every five or six miles. In the full part of the season, which generally coincides with the heaviest fall of rain, with much beating, pulling, and shouting they can scarcely be induced to reach a trot, and may think themselves lucky if they find a change at the end of their stage.

Other means of conveyance for which extra charge is made are landaus and victorias. These, though more comfortable, are heavier for the ponies, and are more difficult to manipulate over bad places in the rainy season.56

Spare baggage and servants can be brought up in the ordinary Indian ekka which, with one pony without changes, takes six to eight days to reach Srinagar; or in bullock carts which take fourteen days.

Tongas will take two, three, four or more days according to the length of the day, the nature of the road, and the disposition of the traveller. The tonga carrying the English mail, travelling almost continuously, covers the distance in thirty-six hours. In the long summer days travellers, starting early, can accomplish the journey in two days.

Every fourteen miles or so is a dak bungalow, where for the payment of one rupee a furnished room is provided, and on further payment meals may be obtained at any time, but "bedding" must always be taken, as nothing but the bare bed is provided.

The stages from Rawal Pindi (1790 feet) at which these bungalows may be found, are:—

Tret	25 ½ miles	25 ½ miles
Sunnybank (6000 feet) (for Murree, 2 miles distant)	11 ¼ "	36 ¾ "
Kohala (2000 feet)	27 ½ "	64 ¼ "
Dulai (2180 feet)	12	76

	"	1/4 "	
Domel (2320 feet)	"	9 1/4 "	85
Garhi (2750 feet)	1/2 "	13 3/4 "	98
Chakoti (3780 feet)	"	21 3/4 "	119
Uri (4425 feet)	1/2 "	13 1/4 "	133
Rampur (4825 feet)	"	13 1/4 "	146
Baramula (5150 feet)	"	16 1/4 "	162
Patan (5200 feet)	1/2 "	16 3/4 "	178
Srinagar (5250 feet)	1/2 "	17 1/4 "	196

57The road is usually open all the year round except in January, February, and part of March, when it is liable to be blocked by snow over the Murree hill and between Rampur and Baramula. In such emergencies the alternative route by Abbotabad may be used, and the traveller must make up his mind to walk the few miles of bad road near Rampur.

Instead of going all the way by road, boat may be taken at Baramula for Srinagar. This, though longer, is much more comfortable and enjoyable. The time occupied is from two to three days.

At Srinagar there is no dak bungalow, but an hotel—Nedou's—which is open the whole year round. Srinagar is the central starting-point for all expeditions. Here house-boats, dunga-boats, camp equipage, and all the paraphernalia of Kashmir travel may be obtained, and shikaris and servants engaged. House-boats are not indigenous to Kashmir. They were introduced by Mr. M. 58T. Kennard some twenty years ago, but now they may be numbered by hundreds. Some are permanently occupied by Europeans, who live in them nearly the whole year round for years together, but most are let out at from Rs. 70 to Rs. 100 per mensem for the season. In midsummer they are hot abodes, but they form a most convenient and luxurious mode of travel. Each would contain, probably, a couple of sitting-rooms with fireplaces, bedrooms, and bath-rooms, and with a cook-boat attached for cooking and servants, the traveller launches forth complete, and either drifts lazily down the river to the many attractive spots along its banks, and to the Wular Lake, or else is towed upwards to Islamabad. The house-boat likewise forms a very convenient base from which short expeditions into the mountains can be made.

Dungas and dunga house-boats are not so luxurious and commodious as the fully developed house-boat; but they are lighter, they travel quicker, and they go up shallow tributaries where the larger boat would stick. They are also less expensive. The former have only loose matting for walls; the walls of the latter are wooden.

For getting about the river in Srinagar itself the still lighter shikara or ordinary paddle-boat 59is used, paddled by two to eight men according to the size. House-boats and dunga house-boats require a crew of six to twelve men. Dungas carry a family in the stern who work the boat. Paddles, poling, and hauling are the means of progression.

Quite good shops for European stores and articles are now springing up in Srinagar. Cox & Co. and the Punjab Banking Co. have branches there, and Cockburn's Agency do every kind of agency work, engage boats and servants, and let out tents, camp furniture, etc. There are also many respectable native firms who do the same—of whom, perhaps, the best is Mohamed Jan, because he does not pester and importune the visitor in the way that most others do, and really render life in Srinagar intolerable.

There is a large choice of expeditions from Srinagar to points of interest, which will be described in detail in a later chapter. First in the immediate vicinity there are picnics to be made to the Dal Lake, to the two Moghal gardens,—the Nishat Bagh and the Shalimar Bagh,—and to the beautiful camping ground of the Nasim Bagh. These are expeditions which can be made in a single afternoon if necessary.60

Of more remote tours the favourites are:—up the river to Islamabad and the beautiful Achibal spring and garden; to the clear crystal springs of Vernag, one of the many sources of the Jhelum; to the famous ruins of Martand which occupy the grandest site for a temple of any in the world; to the Lidar valley, Pahlgam, the Kolahoi glacier, and the caves of Amar Nath. Islamabad is the starting-point for both the Lidar valley and Martand, and here the house-boat may be left. Islamabad, thirty-four miles distant, may also be reached by a road which, though unmetalled, is in dry weather quite good. I have left Srinagar in a motor car at 8.45, have spent over an hour going round Islamabad, have eaten lunch under the glorious chenar trees at Bijbehara, and have been home again at Srinagar by 3.15 the same afternoon.

Down the river are equally delightful tours to be made. At Shadipur, at the junction of the Sind River with the Jhelum River, there is a charming grassy camping-ground under chenar trees. Ganderbal is a few miles higher up the Sind River, and forms the base for expeditions to (1) the Wangat ruins and the Gangarbal Lake, an exquisite torquoise-coloured sheet of water reposing immediately beneath the great cliff and glaciers of the 61Haramokh mountain; and (2) the beautiful Sind valley with its grand mountain scenery, and the charming camping-ground of Sonamarg (the golden meadow) also under towering mountain masses and close to glaciers. Up this valley also lies the road to the Zoji-La Pass on the far side of which branch off roads to Baltistan, on the one hand, with its fine ibex-shooting ground, immense glacier region, and K^2, the second highest mountain in the world; and on the other to Ladak with its Buddhist monasteries perched on any inaccessible rocky pinnacle that can be found, and Leh, the meeting-place of caravans from Lhasa and from Central Asia—a most quaint and picturesque little town embedded among bare, sun-baked mountains which has been the starting-point of two journeys I have made across the dreary, lofty Karakoram Pass (18,500 feet) to Turkestan and to the Pamirs.

From Shadipur, at the junction of the Sind with the Jhelum, the next expedition to be made is to the Wular Lake and Bandipur, from whence ascends immediately the long and numerous zigzags to Tragbal, a favourite camping-ground amid the pines, and to the Tragbal Pass (12,600 feet), from whence a magnificent view of Nanga Parbat (26,600 feet) may be seen, though I am bound to 62say that I have never seen it myself in spite of having crossed the Pass six times on the way to, or returning from, Gilgit and the Hunza frontier which lies in this direction. It is by this route, too, that sportsmen proceeding to shoot markhor in Astor, or ibex and bear in Tilail and Gurais, make their way, as also the few who obtain permission to shoot Ovis Poli on the Pamirs. For myself the Tragbal and Bandipur have many welcome associations, for it is here that I have finished two great exploring expeditions, and on a third occasion returned there after a stay of two and a half years hard service on the Hunza and Chitral frontier. It is impossible to convey the delicious sense of relief the traveller feels in descending from the Pass, in leaving behind all the rigors of severe mountain travel and intense cold, and with each easy step downward feeling the air growing warmer and warmer, and at length reaching the lake throwing himself into an armchair in a comfortable house-boat, and then gliding smoothly over the placid lake with the evening sunlight flooding the beautiful valley, and a soothing sense suffusing him at difficulties surmounted, at hardships past, and at present relaxation of body, mind, and purpose.

THE VALLEY OF GURAIS
CHAPTER III

63

SRINAGAR AND NEIGHBOURHOOD

Entering now into greater detail, first among the places of interest to be described must be Srinagar, the City of the Sun, the capital of the country, and the dwelling-place of 120,000 inhabitants. From both the sanitary and the æsthetic point of view I am always disappointed that Srinagar was not placed either on the plateau of Pariansipura in the centre of the valley, or on the plateau just above Pampur on the west. The former was chosen by the great king Lalataditya for the site of his capital, of which the ruins remain to this day. It is a karewa just opposite the junction of the Sind River with the Jhelum, high and dry above all floods and marshes. And it stands well away from the mountain ranges on either hand, right out in the centre of the valley, so that all the higher peaks and the complete circle of snowy 64mountains may be seen. A nobler site could not be found. The Pampur plateau has the like advantage of being high and dry and healthy, and of being sufficiently raised above the ordinary level of the valley to command views right over the fields and marshes and wooded hamlets; and it also immediately overhangs the river, and commands a view of the most picturesque reaches in its course.

Either of these sites would have been preferable to the present low-lying situation amid the swamps, so muggy in summer and so chill in winter. Yet this site has attractions of its own, and built as it is on either side of the river, with canals and waterways everywhere intersecting it, and with the snowy ranges filling the background of every vista, the city of Srinagar must be ranked among the most beautiful in the East, and in its peculiar style unique.

The distinguishing feature is the combination of picturesque but rickety wooden houses, of mosques and Hindu temples, of balconied shops, of merchants' houses and the royal palaces with the broad sweeping river and the white mountain background.

MARKET BOATS ON THE MAR CANAL, SRINAGAR

Perhaps Srinagar never looks more beautiful than in the fulness of spring towards the end of April, when the Maharaja arrives from Jammu and enters his summer capital by boat. On such occasions the Resident and his staff, all the State officials, and many of the Europeans resident in Srinagar, go by boat to meet His Highness some distance below the city. The Maharaja arrived this year on the most perfect day in spring. Before the time of his arrival the river was alive with craft of every description, from the Resident's state barge of enormous length, and manned by about fifty rowers dressed in scarlet, to light shikaras, and even two motor boats. As we emerged from the town the banks on either side were covered with fresh green grass. The poplars and some magnificent chenar trees overhanging the river were in their freshest foliage. And coming up a long reach of the broad glistening river was the Maharaja's flotilla, with their long lines of red and of blue oarsmen giving colour to the scene.

The two flotillas joined and slowly made their way through the city. On either side were piled up masses of wooden houses, some low, some high, some leaning to one side, some to the other,—none straight and no two alike. All were crowded with people craning at the windows to see the procession. From many hung shawls, the distinctive decoration of the city for state occasions. And most striking and most beautiful feature of all, and only to be seen at this time of year and in Kashmir, the earth-covered roofs were now covered with fresh green grass, with delicate mauve irises, and in some few cases with the gorgeous scarlet Kashmir tulip. A more beautiful object than that of a little mosque on the edge of the river with its chalet-like roof covered with this blaze of scarlet, its graceful spire tapering skywards, its tassel-like bells of brass suspended from the corners all set in a group of overshadowing chenar trees, with the snowy ranges in the far distance, the clear blue sky above and the spring sunshine bathing all in warmth and light, it would be hard indeed to find outside Kashmir.

Beyond the seventh bridge is the Yarkand serai, filled with the Tartar-featured Yarkandis from Central Asia, in whose garb I myself arrived in Srinagar twenty-one years ago, and fully as dark as they from many months' exposure to the sun and snow.

Above this is the first neat, well-constructed buildings—the Zenana hospital built and supported by the State, and now lined by the medical and nursing establishment come out to welcome the Maharaja.

ABOVE THE FIFTH BRIDGE, SRINAGAR

The sixth and most of the other bridges of Srinagar are built up on piers of crossed horizontal logs of wood. They occupy much of the river way, but are very distinctive, and harmonise most picturesquely with the wooden houses of the city. They were all crowded with people. And on the banks near one were assembled many hundreds of school-boys carrying small flags, which they waved as the Maharaja passed, and shouted "Eep, eep, ra! Eep, eep, ra!" continuously for many minutes in imitation of the British cheer. Mottoes of welcome were stretched across the houses in places, some invoking long life for the King-Emperor, and others expressing loyal wishes for the Maharaja. Between the third and fourth bridges are the shops of most of the chief bankers and merchants, big, handsome, picturesque buildings of small bricks and woodwork, with semicircular balconies jutting out over the river and pretty carved and lattice-work windows. Near the third bridge is the fine Shah Hamadan mosque of an almost Norwegian type of architecture, built of wood with a tall taper spire and handsome hanging ornaments from the eaves. Beyond the third bridge is the chief Hindu temple, of quite a different order of architecture, built of stone—and, as along the whole embankment of the river, with the great stone blocks from the temples and cities of ancient Hindu times.

And so the procession up the river continues, through the avenue of houses, mosques, and temples; past rows of grain barges and house-boats tethered to the shores; past the curious wooden bathing-boxes, under the old-style wooden bridge; past flights of steps leading to the water's edge and crowded with people mostly, it is sad to say, in dull brown or the dirtiest white, but sometimes in gay orange-green or purple; past the old residence of the Governors and the new villa of Sir Amar Singh till the Maharaja's palace is reached, where the procession finally halts while all the hundreds of little boats which had followed in rear swarm round the palace steps. The Resident then takes leave, the Maharaja ascends into his palace, and the Resident and the European community proceed still farther up the river to the European settlement in the area known as the Munshi Bagh.

The palace, though large, is disappointing. It is not what one would have expected on such a site. Even the native portion is not handsome, and on to this has been tacked an ugly European edifice. A great chance has been thrown away, and one 69can only hope that time will either tone down the present ungainliness or remove it altogether, and erect a building more worthy of the rulers and of the beautiful country which they rule.

SHAWL MERCHANTS' SHOPS, THIRD BRIDGE, SRINAGAR

On either side are two handsome villas of brick and wood such as are seen on the banks of the Thames; the one belongs to the Maharaja's brother Raja Sir Amar Singh, and the other is allotted by His Highness to his chief spiritual adviser. Beyond is the great flight of steps, at which Lord Minto landed on his arrival in 1906, leading to the main land entrance of the palace on the one hand, and on the other to a new, well-built, fairly clean and extremely picturesque bazaar.

Then the last, or rather, as it is commonly known, the first bridge is passed, over which lies the main road from Rawal Pindi and Baramula to Srinagar and the Munshi Bagh; and beyond this are passed more villas, then the State Hospital and the Museum on the right and various State buildings on the left, including the old Guest House in which were entertained Sir Henry Lawrence and John Nicholson. Beyond is clear of the town, and along the "Bund" or embankment, which forms a lovely walk by the water-edge, has now arisen a series of smart European buildings—the missionaries' quarters, the 70Punjab Bank, Parsi shops, the Post Office, the Residency clerks' quarter and office, and then the Residency itself, a regular English country-house; and beyond it a tidy little Club, the second Assistant Resident's quarters, the Parsonage, the Church, and a line of houses each in its own snug and pretty little garden, the residences of British officials in the employ of the Kashmir State. The whole Bund is overshadowed by great chenar trees and willows, and both sides of the river are lined with house-boats. A thousand feet immediately behind rises the Takht-i-Suliman with the graceful Hindu temple on its summit, and behind this again the great ranges with snow still lying low upon them.

Behind the Bund lie many other modern houses, including Nedou's hotel, and on the slopes of the Takht and towards Gupkar many English villas are springing up—all in much the same style, built of brick and cross-beams of wood with gable roofs. There are also tennis courts and a croquet and badminton grounds round the Club, and on the open plain golf links, a polo ground, and a cricket ground. Srinagar is indeed a gay place for the summer months, with games going on every day, dances nearly every week, dinners, garden parties, and picnics.

MOSQUE OF SHAH HAMADAN, SRINAGAR

71

THE JAMA MASJID

The largest and most striking, though not the most beautiful, of the Mohamedan buildings in Srinagar is the Jama Masjid, which was built by the Emperor Shah Jehan. It is constructed of wood throughout, and is in the form of a square enclosing a courtyard. The main building, of course, faces Mecca. Here there is a forest of pillars all of single deodar trees, and remarkable for their height and grace. A staircase leads on to the roof, from which a good view over the sea of mud-roofed houses of Srinagar may be obtained.

Taken as a whole the building is not very remarkable. The graceful steeples, of the style characteristic of Kashmir, in the centre of each face are worthy of note. But all is in disrepair and neglected, and is hardly worthy of a city of over a hundred thousand Mohamedans.

SHAH HAMADAN MASJID

A more beautiful building than the Jama Masjid is the graceful Mosque of Shah Hamadan, situated close upon the river, and a very favourite object for artists and photographers. It also is built of wood with pointed steeple, beautifully 72carved eaves and hanging bells, like most of the Mohamedan structures in Kashmir.

OTHER BUILDINGS

Scattered throughout the city are other mosques of much the same style of architecture. There are also several Hindu temples of the usual type, and not especially characteristic of Kashmir.

DR. NEVE'S HOSPITAL

Conspicuous above the European quarter stand the group of buildings known all over Kashmir as Dr. Neve's Hospital, a mission hospital which, with Mr. Biscoe's School, is the most sincerely appreciated of all the efforts which Europeans have made for the welfare of the Kashmir people. Last year no less than 22,735 new out-patients were treated, and the total number of visits amounted to 56,280. 1764 in-patients, of whom 476 were females, were also treated; and 5038 surgical operations were performed. Sometimes over 200 out-patients, and on a few days over 300 out-patients, were treated in a single day. These figures speak for themselves.

They show the confidence the people now have in the wonderful institution and the steady practical good it is doing. The heads of the hospital are the brothers Drs. Arthur and Ernest Neve; and they are assisted by Dr. Rawlence, Miss Neve, Miss Robinson, Mr. S. Wilson, and 54 native assistants and servants.

A HINDU TEMPLE, SRINAGAR

The hospital was founded in 1865 by Dr. Elsmie, who for many years had uphill work in starting the institution, but at length gained the confidence of the people and of the late Maharaja. Dr. Downes succeeded Dr. Elsmie, and carried the work forward. In 1881 Dr. Neve took it up. In that year 10,800 new patients were treated; there were 23,393 visits, and 1418 operations were performed. Year by year since then the good work has progressed. The original mud-buildings have gradually been replaced by the present solid masonry structures. And the steady growth of the number of in-patients, and the readiness with which even upper-class women remain in the hospital, testify to the confidence with which the institution is now regarded. It is now renowned through all the north of India, and is a splendid testimony to the steady, thorough, and persevering work of two self-sacrificing men.

THE TAKHT-I-SULIMAN

The most conspicuous object in the neighbourhood of Srinagar is the Takht-i-Suliman, a hill exactly a thousand feet above the valley plain, and surmounted by an ancient Hindu temple. Both for the sake of the view over the valley, up the reaches of the Jhelum, and down on to the Dal Lake and the city of Srinagar immediately at the foot, and also to see the older temple even now frequented by pilgrims from all over India, a climb to the summit is well repaid.

The temple is believed to have been dedicated to Jyesthesvara, a form of the god Siva. It was at one time thought that it was built 220 B.C., but it is now believed by the best authorities that while the massive basement and stairs are remains of an ancient building (possibly Gopaditya's, as Dr. Stein thinks), the present superstructure may be of later date. The roof is certainly modern, but the temple as a whole probably belongs to the same period as the other temples in Kashmir.

It is of the typical Hindu plan of a square with recessed corners, and is built like all the ancient Kashmir temples of massive blocks of stones.

IN THE MAR CANAL, SRINAGAR

PANDRATHAN

Three miles up the river from Srinagar is the site of what is very probably the original city of Srinagar founded by Asoka. The name of Pandrathan now given to the village is identified with the Puranadhisthana, or "ancient capital" of the records, and this has been presumed to be the same as Srinagar founded by Asoka, the Buddhist king. But of this city nothing now remains, and the picturesque temple there is of later date. It was built by the minister Meruvad-dhana in the beginning of the tenth century, and dedicated to Vishnu.

THE DAL LAKE

The Dal Lake, with the canal leading into it, and the various gardens on its shores, is one of the chief attractions of the neighbourhood of Srinagar. It is always lovely, but perhaps at no season more beautiful than early in May. Passing through the lock known as the Dal Darwaza, we glide through channels of still, transparent water hedged in by reeds and willows. On the right rises the Takht-i-Suliman immediately out of the lake. In front are the snowy ranges bordering the Sind valley. Numerous side-channels branch off and intersect. The shores are covered with market gardens. Country boats laden with their produce continually pass, usually propelled by some old man or woman squatting at the extreme prow, and balancing him or herself there with extraordinary confidence and skill. Numerous kingfishers of brilliant sky-blue plumage flash across the water; and gorgeous yellow-golden orioles dart from tree to tree. Clumps of noble chenar trees with the Kashmir chalet houses are grouped along the banks, and often overhang the mirror waters. Orchards of quince trees with their delicate pink and white blossom and fields of brilliant yellow mustard line the shores. Cows and their calves, sheep and their little lambs, graze on the fresh green grass; and pretty but dirty little children, geese and goslings, ducks and ducklings, dabble in the water, and all tell of the rich abundant life now bursting into being.

Rounding a turn in the canal a graceful Hindu temple is seen forming the end of a reach, and on its steps leading to the edge of the water and reflected in it are picturesque groups of women, most of them indeed in the dull brown which they wear with lamentable frequency, but some of them also in bright greens and yellows which furnish the needed touch of colour to the scene.

GUGGRIBAL POINTE ON THE DAL LAKE

Some hundreds of yards farther on we pass under an old bridge with a pointed arch of quaint artistic design of Moghal times. Numerous grain boats of enormous size are congregated here; and half a mile farther the channel gradually opens out, and at length we emerge on to the open lake itself.

The water is so still and so clear that the reflections of the surrounding mountains are seen as in the most polished mirror. The reflected mountain is as sharp and distinct as the mountain itself. The luxuriant plant growth from the bottom and the numerous fishes are seen as in clear air. On the far shores of the lake the stately avenues of the Nishat and Shalimar Baghs approach the water's edge. Above them rise high mountain cliffs. Graceful boats glide smoothly over the glassy surface of the lake—some the bearers of market produce, some occupied by fishermen, and a few filled with holiday-makers enjoying thoroughly the beauty of the scene, and giving expression to the enjoyment in songs and music.

May is not the season for the lotus, so that one additional attraction is lacking; but in July and August, when the lotus is in full bloom, the lake itself, though not the shores and setting, is at perfection. The lotuses are as large as the two hands joined together, of a delicate pink, and set on the water in hundreds. In the midst of their graceful leaves they add a beauty to the lake which attracts multitudes from the city.

Gliding on beyond the lotuses we pass the famous Isle of Chenars with its magnificent trees and grassy velvet banks; we pass a little promontory with another huge chenar tree growing out right over the water, and giving shelter to a house-boat comfortably ensconced beneath its shade; and then we reach the widest and most open portion of the lake. In the distance, towards the Sind valley, well-wooded villages cover the lower slopes of the mountains inclining towards the lake, and away in the farthest westward distance the Khagan snows are faintly traced.

From here to the Nishat or Shalimar Baghs we would bear off to the right. To the Nasim Bagh we bear to the left, and closing in to the southern shore pass a picturesque village by the side of the lake with chalet-like house, a handsome ziarat, a background of chenar trees and long lines of steps, generally crowded with people, leading to the water's edge. In about an hour's row from the start at the Dal Darwaza the Nasim Bagh is reached.

LOTUS LILIES ON THE DAL LAKE

NASIM BAGH

The Nasim Bagh is a series of avenues of glorious chenar trees crossing one another at right angles, and each avenue about three hundred yards in length. Under these is soft, fresh green grass, and the whole is raised twenty or thirty feet above the water. There are no flower gardens, but the site makes a perfect camping-ground, and many house-boats anchor here in the summer.

Looking out from the shade of the chenars we see straight across the lake the Shalimar Bagh with the Dachigan valley behind it, and the snowy Mahadeo Peak towering above. From the opposite side of the Bagh, looking away from the lake, there are views over the Kashmir valley to the snows of the Pir Panjal and of the Khagan range. And round the edges were clumps of large white and purple irises.

In the autumn the Nasim Bagh is more beautiful still, for then the chenars are in all the richness of their autumn foliage, and a more perfect camping or picnic spot man could hardly wish for.

THE SHALIMAR BAGH

On the north-east corner of the Dal Lake, and approached by a canal about a mile in length, with banks of soft green turf, and running between an avenue of chenars and willows, is the Shalimar Bagh, or royal garden, the favourite resort of the Moghal Emperor Jehangir and his wife, the famous Nurmahal, for whom the Taj at Agra was built as a tomb. The gardens can also be reached by a beautiful road along the shores of the lake, nine miles from the city of Srinagar.

The situation is not so beautiful as the site of the Nishat Bagh, for it is almost on a level, and is surrounded by a high wall. But it is only in comparison with the Nishat Bagh that it can suffer disparagement, and anywhere else than in Kashmir it would be hard to find a more beautiful garden than the Shalimar on an autumn evening, when the great avenue of chenar trees is tinged with gold and russet, when the lofty mountains which rise behind it take on every shade of blue and purple, and the long lines of fountains running through the avenue sparkle in the sunshine.

SHALIMAR GARDENS

The garden is remarkable too for a pavilion, with exquisitely carved pillars of black marble. It is set in a tank in which play numbers of fountains, and round the borders of the tank are massive chenar trees. The total length of the garden is 600 yards, and it is arranged in four terraces, on three of which 81are pavilions. Except for the pavilion with marble pillars and the water channel, the garden is in a state of ruin; but Mr. Nichols of the Archæological Department Survey has attempted to reconstruct its former outlines. There is a tradition that the garden was originally larger than the present walled enclosure, and there are found along the canal which connects it with the Dal Lake the ruins of masonry foundations, which mark either the beginning of the old garden or the site of a pavilion within it. Causeways and channels probably extended across the garden with tanks and platforms.

The garden was in the strictest sense a formal garden, and in making his recommendation for its restoration, Mr. Nichols enlarges on the artificiality which is the charm of a formal garden. Appreciation of a formal garden requires, he thinks, an acquired taste, but the Moghals certainly understood such matters. They were quite right in selecting trees of formal growth, and planting them on geometrical lines, the essence of a good garden being that it should form a pleasing intermediate step between the free treatment which Nature lavishes on hills and plains, field and forest, and that necessarily artificial object—a building made by the hand of men.82

Such are Mr. Nichols' ideas, for which there is a good deal to be said. But some may also think that when a once formal garden and formal buildings have *already* fallen into ruin and returned as it were to nature, there may be less need to restore the formality, and that to fall in with the ways of Nature may be the best method of adding to the existing beauty of the garden. In any case the improvement of the turf, the removal of modern hideosities of buildings, and the replacing of the makeshift fountains by fountains of really tasteful design, would greatly improve this beautiful garden.

THE NISHAT BAGH

The Nishat Bagh is decidedly the favourite garden in Kashmir, though it has no building so fine as the pavilion with the black pillars in the Shalimar Bagh. Its situation on the rising ground sloping up from the Dal Lake, backed by a range of mountains immediately behind, and with views far over the water and over the valley to the distant snowy mountains, gives it an advantage over every other garden, and its beauty in spring-time when the Kashmir lilac and the fruit trees are in blossom, when the chenars are in young 83leaf and the turf in its freshest green, I have already described.[1] In the autumn it is scarcely less beautiful in a different way. Then the chenars are in a gorgeous foliage of gold and purple. Day after day of brilliant sunshine and cloudless sky give a sense of security of beauty, and no more perfect pleasure-ground could be imagined.

THE NISHAT BAGH

The garden was constructed by the Moghal Emperor Jehangir. It can be reached either by water or by road along the shores of the lake. It is about 600 yards long and divided into seven terraces, each rising well above the other. Down the centre runs a water-channel broken into a succession of waterfalls and fountains, and shaded by an avenue of chenars.

The pavilion at the entrance, though affording from its upper story a striking view of the garden right up the line of waterfalls and fountains, and on to the mountains which hang over the garden, is a modern structure and is not beautiful in itself. It is a thousand pities, indeed, that this most superb site has not been made use of to construct a really beautiful pavilion on the lines of that in the Shalimar Bagh. On the higher terraces are 84the foundations of other pavilions and massive stone throne-like seats which indicate the fuller beauties of the Moghal times.

On the topmost terrace is a beautiful clump of magnificent chenar trees and a wide extent of soft green turf—an ideal spot for picnics and garden-parties. And it is from this point that can be seen the most beautiful and extensive views through the avenue of chenar trees, over the fountains and waterfalls, on to the glassy lake and the distant snowy ranges.

PARIHASAPURA

A very little known but very accessible and particularly interesting spot is the site of the ancient city of Parihasapura, the modern Paraspur, situated two and a half miles south-west of Shadipur, and stretching from there on a karewa, or raised plateau, to the Srinagar and Baramula road. There is not much left now above ground, for numbers of the massive blocks of stone of which the city and temples were built have been taken away ages ago to build the temples of Patan close by, and, alas! also to metal the Baramula road. But the outlines of the walls may still be traced sufficiently well to attest the grand scale 85on which the city was built; and we know from records that it was built by the same great king Lalatadityta, who erected the temple of Martand in the eighth century.

A TERRACE OF THE NISHAT BAGH

And Parihasapura, like Martand, has been set off to the greatest advantage by natural scenery. This Kashmir king must indeed have been worthy of the beautiful country which he ruled. In his time the Sind and Jhelum rivers met, not at Shadipur as now, but at the edge of the karewa on which Lalataditya built his city. And from the plateau views could be obtained right up the Sind valley to Haramukh and the craggy mountain peaks which bound it on either side; far up and down the main valley, over the fields of emerald rice or golden mustard, and the numerous hamlets hidden in clumps of chenar and willow, mulberry and walnut; over also the glistening reaches of the Jhelum River, to the snowy ranges which at a distance far enough away not to dwarf or overpower the city encircled it on every side. No temple was ever built on a finer site than Martand, and no city was ever set in more lovely surroundings than Parihasapura.

According to a passage in the Rajatarangini the king Lalataditya erected five large buildings: 86(1) a temple of Vishnu Parihasakesava with a silver image; (2) a temple of Vishnu Muktakesava with a golden image; (3) a temple of Vishnu Mahavaraha with an image clad in golden armour; (4) a temple to the god Govardhanadhara with a silver image; (5) the Rajavihara or monastery with a large quadrangle and a colossal statue of Buddha in copper, which indicate that in ancient times there must have been a large and important Buddhist settlement. The same king is also said to have erected a stone pillar 54 cubits high with an image of Garuda on the top.

CHAPTER IV
87

THE RESIDENCY GARDEN

Among the beauties of Kashmir the Residency Garden must surely not be omitted. The Maharaja has provided for the Residency one of the most charming houses in India—a regular English country-house. And successive Residents, in my case aided by Mr. Harrison and Major Wigram, have striven to make the garden worthy of the country and the house. Here grows in perfection every English flower. The wide lawns are as soft and green as any English lawn. All the English fruits—pears, apples, peaches, apricots, plums, greengages, cherries, walnuts, mulberries, gooseberries, currants, raspberries, and strawberries—grow to perfection and in prodigious quantities; and the magnificent chenar and innumerable birds add a special charm of their own.

Perhaps a record of the cycle of the birds 88and flowers will give an idea not only of the beauties of the garden, but of the climate of the valley.

Early in March the garden beauties begin to develop. The turf is then still quite brown and the trees leafless, but on March 8th, when I returned to Srinagar this year, violets, pansies, wall-flowers, narcissus, crocuses, and daisies were all in flower. Daffodils, hyacinths, stock and a few carnations were in bud. Columbine and larkspur leaves were sprouting. Peas and broad beans sown in November were a few inches high. And of the trees, willow leaf-buds were just bursting and showing a tinge of fresh light yellow green, and one apricot tree was nearly bursting into blossom. Of birds there were thrushes, minas, bulbuls, sparrows, crows, kites, blue-tits, hoopoes, and starlings; and of butterflies, a few tortoise-shell and cabbage-whites.

The maximum temperature in the shade was 55° and in the sun 104°, and the minimum temperature was 31°.

On March 17th the willow trees had acquired a distinct tinge of green, as also had the grass. Wild hyacinths (blue-bells) and yellow crocuses were well out. The maximum temperature was 8968° in the shade and 110° in the sun, and the minimum was 32°.

THE RESIDENCY AND CLUB, SRINAGAR

On the same day in the previous year the maximum was 56° and the minimum 35°, and four days later there was snow.

By March 20th the apricot blossoms were in full bloom. Willow trees were in half-leaf. Garden hyacinths, daffodils, Crown Imperials, and English primroses were just beginning to bloom; and greengages were in blossom.

By the end of March the maximum temperature had reached 75° in the shade and 125° in the sun, while the minimum stood at 40°. This, however, was an exceptionally warm March.

By April 1st the garden was exquisitely beautiful. The willows were now well out, and in all the charm of fresh young spring foliage. Apricots and peach trees formed little clouds of delicate pink and white dotted lightly over the garden, and not too dense to hide the glories of the snowy mountains in the background. The tall pear trees were nearly in full bloom. A few of the pinky-white apple blossoms were just appearing. The May leaves were showing a tinge of green. Chenar leaves were just appearing. The mulberry leaf-buds were beginning to burst. Catkins were 90hanging from the poplars. Rose leaves were fully out. The grass had nearly turned from brown to green. Iris buds were showing a tinge of purple. Hyacinths were well out, and Crown Imperials and daffodils in full bloom.

On April 3rd the first of the pretty little wild tulips striped white and pink appeared, and on the following day the first of the large dark purple irises and two or three large white irises came into bloom. Heavy rain fell, and on the 5th the grass was entirely green. On that day the pears were in full blossom. Two of the magnificent scarlet Kashmir tulips, which are a joy to any garden, came into blossom, and two English tulips also came out. Rose-buds were beginning to form. The maximum temperature was 59° and the minimum 42°. On April 7th the first columbine came into bloom, and on the 9th the first shrike appeared.

Now followed a deluge of rain. On the 12th 2½ inches fell. By the morning of the 13th 14·65 inches had fallen since January 1st, in comparison with a normal fall of 10·6 inches. And, most unexpected of all, on the night of 12th-13th snow fell! The maximum temperature was only 50° and the minimum 33°. In a single night all the lovely 91delicate peach blossoms, the crowning glory of the Kashmir spring, were withered up, and for the moment we seemed plunged back once more to winter.

But April 15th was one of Kashmir's most lovely days. The poplars were now in fresh light foliage. May was in full leaf. Irises were plentiful. Several columbines were in bloom. Both the Kashmir and English tulips were well out; and the strawberries were in blossom. On this day, too, I saw a flight of green parrots with long yellow tails in the garden.

The first rose bloomed on April 17th, a white climber whose name I do not know, growing on the south verandah. Last year the first did not appear till the 26th.

May came into bloom on April 24th, and on the 25th a scarlet poppy and a white peony blossomed. For some days then the weather had been exceptionally warm, the maximum rising to 80° in the shade and 129° in the sun, and the minimum to 51°.

The first golden oriole appeared on the 26th—exactly the same date as that on which it appeared last year. The golden orioles have a glorious deep liquid note which thrills through the whole 92garden. Two or three pairs always settle there, and all day long their brilliant yellow plumage is seen flashing from tree to tree.

Three days later another brilliant visitant appears, the paradise fly-catcher. He has not the beautiful note of the golden oriole, nor such striking plumage. But he has exceedingly graceful form and movements. He has a very long, wavy, ribbony tail, like a paradise bird, and the two or three pairs of them which yearly settle in the garden may be seen at any hour undulating through the foliage or darting swiftly out to catch their prey.

By May 1st the magnificent chenar trees were in full leaf. Mulberry, horse-chestnut, and walnut were also well in leaf. The roses were coming into bloom—numerous Maréchal Neil, and a beautiful single pink rose—the sinica anemone—a few of Fortune's yellow, and many tea-roses. The May trees were in full blossom. The bank on the south side of the garden was a mass of dark purple and white irises, and of an evening when the sunlight glancing low along its length caused each flower to stand out in separate state, became a blaze of glory. Another beauty of this season were bushes of what is generally known as Indian May, with long slender stalks bent 93gracefully downward like a waterfall of snowy flowers. Stock was in full bloom. Pansies were out in masses. Both the English and Kashmir lilac were in blossom, and the columbines were in perfection. I had hold out from Barr & Sons a number of varieties, and the success was remarkable. The Kashmir soil and climate seem to suit columbines, and varieties from every part of the world, deep purple, light mauve, white, mauve and white, pink and red of many different graceful forms, came up luxuriantly. They were one of the successes which gladden an amateur gardener's heart.

The maximum in the shade was 60°, in the sun 122°, and the minimum 48°.

The first strawberries ripened a week later. The first horse-chestnuts came into blossom on May 10th, and on that date the single pink rose, sinica anemone, on the trellis at the end of the garden, was in full bloom and of wondrous beauty; a summer-house covered with Fortune's yellow was a dream of golden loveliness; I picked the first bloom of some English roses which a kind friend had sent out, and which had been planted in a special rose garden I had made for them—William Shean, Mrs. Ed. Mauley, Mrs. W. J. Grant, and 94Carmine Pillar; and we had our first plateful of strawberries.

A light mauve iris, a native of Kashmir, now came into bloom; geraniums and some lovely varieties of Shirley poppy which I had obtained from Mr. Luther Burbank, the famous plant-breeder of California, began to blossom; and roses of every variety came rapidly on till the garden became a blaze of colour.

The first of some remarkably beautiful delphiniums—some a deep blue, some sky blue, and some opalescent—which I had also obtained from Luther Burbank appeared in bloom on May 17th.

A spell of hot weather now set in, and on May 21st the maximum temperature rose to 84° in the shade and 134° in the sun, and the minimum to 54°.

THE TAKHT-I-SULIMAN, FROM THE RESIDENCY GARDEN

By May 25th the roses were at their maximum of beauty. The sweetly-scented and delicately-coloured La France roses were at perfection. Rich bushes of General Jacqueminot, of John Hopper, of the pink rose of Kashmir, and of many other kinds whose names I do not know, formed great masses of colour against the soft green leaves and the plentiful foliage of the chenar trees. William Alan Richardson climbed over the trellises. The Shirley poppies gave every deep or delicate shade of red and pink. Sweet-peas were in full bloom, and of them also I had had a marvellous variety from England. Pinks and carnations were coming rapidly on. A mauve and yellow iris had appeared. Luther Burbank's delphiniums formed welcome patches of real true blues in the herbaceous border round the lawn. The light and graceful gypsophylis and phlox were in bloom; gladioli were just coming out; and the horse-chestnut trees were all in gorgeous blossom.

Early in June the gladioli, Canterbury bells, pinks, sweet-williams, and foxgloves were in full bloom, and the sweet-william especially gave masses of beautiful and varied colour. The temperature now rose to 88° in the shade and 135° in the sun, and the minimum to 54°. On June 10th, carnations, phlox, and Eschscholtzia were in full bloom. And by June 15th, though many of the best roses had passed over two beautiful climbers which I had obtained from home, Dorothy Perkins and Lady Gay were in full blossom, and the delicate pink and graceful form of the latter were especially lovely. Geraniums and fuschias were now fully out, and masses of tall hollyhocks in many different shades of colour were most effective. A few cannas and some lilies also came into bloom.

By the end of June apricots were ripe. Petunias and dahlias were out, and a few columbines still remained in bloom. The temperature had now gone up to 94° in the shade and 142° in the sun, and the minimum to 62°; and early in July it rose to 97° in the shade, which is about as hot as it ever becomes in the valley.

On returning to Srinagar on September 7th I found the bed of scarlet salvias giving brilliant patches of colour and most effectively lighting up the garden. The autumn crop of roses was beginning, though the blooms were not so fine as the spring crop. Geraniums, fuschias, asters, cannas, zinnias, gallardia, and verbena were in abundance; stock and phlox were still out, and the hibiscus bushes were in full bloom. Burbank's delphiniums were also having a light second bloom. The maximum in the shade was 81° and in the sun 128°, and the minimum 52°. The rainfall to date from January 1st was 27·4 inches in comparison with a normal fall of 21·7 inches.

By the beginning of October last year cosmos was blooming luxuriantly. Christmas roses were in full blossom, and the first chrysanthemum appeared. During the month these blossomed in great beauty and became the chief attraction in the garden. Towards the end of the month and beginning of November the great chenar trees gradually assumed the gorgeous autumn colouring. The Virginian creeper on the porch turned to every rich hue of red and purple. Then the glories of the garden slowly vanished away. The leaves fell from the trees. The frost turned the turf brown. On December 1st there were still a few brave remnants of the summer splendour—a few tea-roses, stocks, phlox, wallflower, chrysanthemums, carnations, petunias, gallardia, nasturtiums, salvia, snapdragons, and one or two violets. But the temperature was now 25° at night, and the maximum in the day only 54°, and these too soon disappeared, and the only consolation left was the clearer view of the mountains of which the absence of foliage on the trees allowed. Thus ends the story of a garden's glory.

CHAPTER V

GULMARG

What will be one day known as the playground of India, and what is known to the Kashmiris as the "Meadow of Flowers," is situated twenty-six miles from Srinagar, half-way up the northward-facing slopes of the Pir Panjal. There is no other place like Gulmarg. Originally a mere meadow to which the Kashmiri shepherds used to bring their sheep, cattle, and ponies for summer grazing, it is now the resort of six or seven hundred European visitors every summer. The Maharaja has a palace there. There is a Residency, an hotel, with a theatre and ball-room, post office, telegraph office, club, and more than a hundred "huts" built and owned by Europeans. There are also golf links, two polo grounds, a cricket ground, four tennis courts, and two croquet grounds. There are level circular roads running all round it. There is a pipe water-supply, and maybe soon there will be electric light everywhere. And yet for eight months in the year the place is entirely deserted and under snow.

Like Kashmir generally, Gulmarg also is said by those who knew it in the old days to be now "spoilt." With the increasing numbers of visitors, with the numerous huts springing up year by year in every direction, with the dinners and dances, it is said to have lost its former charms, and it is believed that in a few years it will not be worth living in. My own view is precisely the opposite. I knew Gulmarg nineteen years ago, and it certainly then had many charms. The walks and scenery and the fresh bracing air were delightful. Where now are roads there were then only meandering paths. What is now the polo ground was then a swamp. The "fore" of the golfer was unknown. All was then Arcadian simplicity. Nothing more thrilling than a walk in the woods, or at most a luncheon party, was ever heard of.

And, doubtless, this simplicity of life has its advantages. But it had also its drawbacks. Man cannot live for ever on walks however charming and however fascinating his companion may be. His soul yearns for a ball of some kind whether it 100be a polo ball, a cricket ball, a tennis ball, a golf ball, or even a croquet ball. Until he has a ball of some description to play with he is never really happy.

So now that a sufficient number of visitors come to Gulmarg to supply subscriptions enough to make and keep up really good golf links, polo grounds, etc., I for my part think Gulmarg is greatly improved. I think, further, that it has not yet reached the zenith of its attractions. It is the Gulmarg of the future that will be the really attractive Gulmarg, when there is money enough to make the second links as good as the first, to lay out good rides down and around the marg, to make a lake at the end, to stock it with trout, and to have electric light and water in all the "huts," and when a good hotel and a good club, with quarters for casual bachelor visitors, have been built.

ON THE CIRCULAR ROAD, GULMARG

All this is straying far from the original Arcadian simplicity, but those who wish for simplicity can still have it in many another valley in Kashmir—at Sonamarg, Pahlgam, or Tragbal, and numerous other places, and the advantage of Gulmarg is that the visitor can still if he choose be very fairly simple. He can go about in a suit 101of puttoo. He need not go to a single dance, or theatrical performance, or dinner-party, or play a single game. He need not speak to a soul unless he wants to. He can pitch his tent in some remote end of the marg, and he can take his solitary walks in the woods; *but*, if after a while he finds his own society is not after all so agreeable as he had thought, if he feels a hankering for the society of his fellows, male or female, and if he finds the temptation to play with some ball is irresistible, then just under his nose is every attraction. He can indulge his misanthropic inclinations at will, and at a turn in those inclinations he can plunge into games and gaiety to his heart's content.

The main charm of Gulmarg will, however, always remain the beauty of its natural scenery and the views of the great peak, Nanga Parbat, 26,260 feet above sea-level, and 80 miles distant across the valley. The marg or meadow itself is a flowery, saucer-shaped hollow under a mountain 13,000 feet high, and bounded by a ridge directly overhanging the main valley of Kashmir. It is 8500 feet above sea-level, open and covered with flowers and soft green turf, but on all sides it is surrounded by forests of silver fir interspersed 102with spruce, blue pine, maple, and a few horse-chestnuts, and the great attraction is that through this forest of stately graceful firs the most superb views may be had, first over the whole length and breadth of the vale of Kashmir, then along the range of snowy mountains on the north, and as a culminating pleasure, to the solitary Nanga Parbat, which stands out clear and distinct above and beyond all the lesser ranges, and belonging, so it seems, to a separate and purer world of its own. And there is the further attraction in the Gulmarg scenery that it is ever changing—now clear and suffused in brilliant sunlight, now the battle-ground of monsoon storms, and now again streaked with soft fleecy vapours and bathed in haze and colour. No two days are alike, and each point of view discloses some new loveliness.

Round the outside of the ridge runs what is known as the circular road. It has the advantage of being perfectly level, and is fit for riding as well as walking. Except the road through the tropical forests near Darjiling, along which I rode on my way to and from Tibet, and which runs for miles through glorious tropical vegetation, by immense broad-leaved trees with unknown names, all festooned with creepers and lighted with orchids; 103by great tree ferns, wild bananas, and a host of other treasures of plant life, and through which glimpses of the mighty Kinchinjanga, 28,250 feet, could be caught,—except that I know of no other more beautiful road than this along the ridge of Gulmarg.

IN THE FOREST

From it one looks down through the wealth of forest on to the valley below, intersected with streams and water-channels, dotted over with wooded villages, and covered with rice-fields of emerald green; on to the great river winding along the length of the valley to the Wular Lake at its western end; on to the glinting roofs of Srinagar; on to the snowy range on the far side-valley; and, finally, on to Nanga Parbat itself.

And never for two days together is this glorious panorama exactly the same. One day the valley will be filled with a sea of rolling clouds through which gleams of sunshine light up the brilliant green of the rice-fields below. Above the billowy sea of clouds long level lines of mist will float along the opposite mountain-sides. Above these again will rise the great mountains looking inconceivably high. And above all will soar Nanga Parbat, looking at sunset like a pearly island rising from an ocean of ruddy light.

On another day there will be not a cloud in the sky. The whole scene will be bathed in a bluey haze. Through the many vistas cut in the forest the eye will be carried to the foot-hills sloping gradually towards the river, to the little clumps of pine wood, the village clusters of walnut, pear, and mulberry, the fields of rice and maize, to the silvery reaches of the Jhelum, winding from the Wular Lake to Baramula, to the purply blue of the distant mountains, then on to the bluey white of Nanga Parbat, sharply defined, yet in colour nearly merging into the azure of the sky, and showing out in all the greater beauty that we see it framed by the dark and graceful pines in which we stand.

And this forest has no mean attractions of its own, of which to my little girl the chief were the white columbines. Here also are found purple columbines, delphiniums, what are known as white slipper orchids, yellow violets, balsams, mauve and yellow primulas, potentillas, anemones, Jacob's ladder, monkshood, salvias, many graceful ferns, and numerous other flowers of which I do not pretend to know the name.

FROM THE CIRCULAR ROAD, GULMARG

The Residency is situated on the summit of the ridge above the circular road, and from it can be seen not only Nanga Parbat (through a vista cut in the trees) and the main valley, but also a lovely little side-valley known as the Ferozepur nulla. Looking straight down two thousand feet through the pine trees we see a mountain torrent whose distant rumbling mingles soothingly with the sighing of the pines. Brilliant green meadows, on which a few detached pine trees stand gracefully out here and there, line the river banks. Steep hill-sides, mostly clad in gloomy forest, rise on either hand, but relieved by many patches of grassy sun-lit slope. The spurs become a deeper and deeper purple as they recede. The openings in the forests become wider higher on the mountain-side where the avalanches have scoured them more frequently. Higher still the forest-line is passed, and the little stream is seen issuing from its source among the snow-fields and flowing over enticing grassy meadows. Above the glistening snow-fields rises a rugged peak of the Pir Panjal which, when it is not set against a background of intense blue sky, is the butt of raging storm-clouds.

The most beautiful time in Gulmarg is in September, when the rains are over and the first fresh autumn nip is in the air. Then from the summer-house in our garden, in the early morning, to feast my eyes on Nanga Parbat was a perpetual delight. It was the very emblem of purity, dignity, and repose. Day after day it would appear as a vision of soft pure white in a gauze-like haze of delicate blue. Too light and too ethereal for earth, but seemingly a part of heaven; a vision which was a religion in itself, which diffused its beauty throughout one's being, and evoked from it all that was most pure and lovely.

The foreground in this autumn month was also worthy of the supreme subject of the picture. Through the pines the touches of sunlit meadow, fresh and green, with long shadows of the trees thrown here and there across them and intensifying the effect of the sunlight; the groups of cattle; the horizontal streaks of mist floating on the edge of the woods; the cheerful twittering of the birds; the soothing hum of the bees and insects; the crowing of cocks; the rippling sound of running water; and then, looking towards Aparwat, the brilliant sunshine brightening the emerald grass of the marg; the patches of yellow flowers; the little meandering stream; the pretty chalet huts peeping out from the edge of the trees; the background of dark firs and pines getting lighter as they merge into the bluey haze of the distance; the fresh green meadows over the limit of the pines; the snow-fields; the rocky peaks, and above all the clear blue liquid sky,—all this gave a setting and an atmosphere which fitly served as an accompaniment to this most impressive of Nature's works.

CHAPTER VI

THE VALLEYS AND PLACES OF INTEREST

THE SIND VALLEY

The most bold and striking of the side-valleys is undoubtedly the Sind valley. A fourteen-miles' ride, or a night in a boat, takes the traveller to Ganderbal at its mouth, from which

Sonamarg, the favourite camping-ground near the head of the valley, is four marches distant. The lower portion is not particularly interesting, though even here the pine woods, the rushing river, and the village clusters are beautiful. But at Sonamarg—"the golden meadow"—the great peaks close round, glaciers pour down from them almost on to the camping-ground, and the scenery has all the grandeur of the Alps.

GORGE OF THE SIND VALLEY AT GUGGANGIR

Sonamarg itself is a narrow grassy flat, 8650 feet above sea-level, extending for some two miles between the hill-side and the river bank where 109another beautiful valley joins in from the south-west. All the slopes and meadows are covered with alpine flowers. Rich forests of silver fir, intermingled with sycamore and fringed on their upper borders with silver birch, clothe the mountain-sides. From each valley flows a rich white glacier. Grand rocky cliffs encircle the forests and meadows, and culminate in bold snowy peaks which give a crowning beauty to the whole. It is an ideal camping-ground and a strong rival to Gulmarg.

Some fifteen miles beyond Sonamarg is the Zoji-la Pass leading to Ladak and Baltistan. It was by this pass that I first entered Kashmir in 1887, and coming thus from the opposite direction, the change in scenery was most remarkable. For hundreds of miles from the northern side I had traversed country which though of the grandest description, was absolutely devoid of forest. The great mountains, sublime in their ruggedness and in the purity of their snowy mantle, were yet completely barren. Then, of a sudden, as I crossed the Zoji-la all was changed in a moment, and I burst into one of the loveliest valleys in the world with glorious forests clothing every slope. It was a refreshing and delightful change, a relaxation from a sublimity too stern to bear for long, to the 110homely geniality of earthly life, and the remembrance of it still lies fresh upon my memory.

GANGABAL LAKE

About forty miles from Srinagar, and lying at the foot of the great peak Haramokh, is the remarkable Gangabal Lake. It is reached by a steep pull of 4000 feet from the Sind valley. By the side of the path rushes a clear, ice-cold stream. From the top of the rise are superb views precipitously down to the Wangat valley leading up from the Sind and beyond it to a jagged range of spires and pinnacles. The path then leads over rolling downs, covered in summer with ranunculus and primulas, to a chain of torquoise and ice-green lakes, above which grimly towers the massive Haramokh six thousand feet above the water, and giving birth to voluminous glistening glaciers which roll down to the water's edge.

It is a silent, solitary, and impressive spot, and is held in some reverence by the Hindus.

THE FROZEN LAKE, GANGABAL
THE LOLAB

The Lolab is the western end of the vale of Kashmir, and is remarkable rather for the homely 111picturesqueness of its woodland and village beauty than for the grandeur of its scenery. It is usually reached by boat up the Pohru River three miles below Sopur. In two days the limit of navigation at Awatkula is reached. From thence the road leads to Kofwara, eight miles, and Lalpura, the chief place, twelve miles farther. The hill-sides are entirely clothed with thick forests of deodar and pine. In the valley bottom are beautiful stretches of soft green turf. Dotted over it are villages buried in park-like clumps of walnut, apple, and pear trees; and numerous streams ripple through on every side. For forest and village scenery it is nowhere excelled. It is like a series of English woodland glades, with the additional beauty of snowy peaks in the background.

THE LIDAR VALLEY

A favourite side-valley is the Lidar, for which the road takes off from the main valley at Bijbehara. It is not of such wild rocky grandeur as the Sind valley, but has milder beauties of its own, charming woodland walks, and in summer a wealth of roses pink and white, jasmine, forget-me-nots, a handsome spiræa, strawberry, honeysuckle, 112etc. By the side of the road runs the cool, foaming Lidar stream, and everywhere are villages hidden amongst masses of chenar, walnut, and mulberry.

On the left bank one and a half miles from Islamabad is the famous spring of Bawan—a great tank under cool chenar trees. The spring is sacred to Vishnu, and is in the charge of Brahmins, who keep a book in which visitors have inscribed their names since 1827. The tank is full of fishes fed by the Brahmins, and thousands dash to catch the bread when thrown into the water. Altogether the village and the cool spring welling out of the mountain-side, and the whole shaded by magnificent old chenar trees, form a most attractive spot well worth a visit.

Twenty-four miles from Bijbehara, or twenty-eight from Islamabad, is Pahlgam, always the camping-ground of several visitors during the summer. Here, too, Colonel Ward for many years has resided in the summer in a small house built by himself, but now taken over by the State. I fancy life here is dull compared with life at Gulmarg, but for those who wish to vegetate and lead an absolutely quiet existence Pahlgam is admirably suited. It is two thousand feet higher than Srinagar. The 113camping-ground is in a wood of blue pines, and the fresh, clear, pine-scented air is refreshing after the stuffy main valley in midsummer.

EARLY MORNING NEAR PAHLGAM, LIDAR VALLEY

Above Pahlgam the valley bifurcates, one branch going to Aru, by which a road leads over a troublesome pass into the Sind valley; and the other leading to Shisha Nag and to the famous caves of Amarnath, the resort of many hundreds of pilgrims in July and August. Immediately beyond Pahlgam, on this latter route, the path leads through beautiful woods with fine views of rocky heights and snowy peaks. Numerous maiden-hair and other ferns, primulas, crane's bill, gentians, and many other well-known flowers line the road-side. Above the wood line are fine grassy uplands frequented by Gujars with their cattle, ponies, buffaloes, sheep, and goats. Lidarwat is a lovely camping-ground in a green lawn fringed by a deep belt of trees. Beyond is the Kolahoi glacier, the road to which leads over a wide and treeless valley, and in places crosses snow bridges. The camping-ground is 11,000 feet above sea-level, and is set in a circle of stately peaks. The end of the glacier is of grey ice, and so strewn over with fragments of grey rock as hardly to be recognisable as ice, though the ice is, in fact, two hundred feet thick. Above 114it rises the bold peak of Kolahoi, so conspicuous in its sharp needle form from Gulmarg, and six thousand feet above the glacier.

The cave of Amarnath is about 41 miles from Pahlgam, and is about 13,000 feet above sea-level. It is therefore above all tree vegetation, and is set in wild and impressive scenery. The cave itself is of gypsum, and is fifty yards long by fifty broad at the mouth, and thirty at the centre. Inside is a frozen spring which is the object of worship, and beside it is a noble glacier and bold and rugged cliffs.

MARTAND

Of all the ruins in Kashmir the Martand ruins are both the most remarkable and the most characteristic. No temple was ever built on a finer site. It stands on an open plain, where it can be seen to full advantage. Behind it rises a range of snowy mountains. And away in the distance before it, first lies the smiling Kashmir valley, and then the whole length of the Pir Panjal range, their snowy summits mingling softly with the azure of the sky. It is one of the most heavenly spots on earth, not too grand to be 115overpowering, nor too paltry to be lacking in strength and dignity, and it is easy to understand the impulse which led a people to here raise a temple to heaven.

THE RUINS OF MARTAND

The temple of Martand is the finest example of what is known as the Kashmirian style of architecture, and was built by the most noted of the Kashmir kings, Lalataditya, who reigned between the years 699 and 736 A.D.

Apart from its site it cannot be considered one of the really great ruins of the world; but yet there is about it a combination of massiveness and simplicity, and of solidity combined with grace, which have earned it fame for a thousand years. There is something of the rigidity and strength of the Egyptian temples, and something of the grace of the buildings of Greece. Yet it is neither so Egyptian nor so Grecian as the one or the other. Though Hindu, it differs from the usual Hindu types; and is known distinctively as Kashmirian. It is, however, decidedly Hindu, and not either Buddhist or Jain, and owes much to the influence of Gandhara, while the sculptures show, according to Marshal, a close connection with the typical Hindu work of the late Gupta period.116

ACHIBAL

At the eastern end of the valley is another of the Moghal gardens, at the spot where quite a little river comes gushing straight out of the mountain-side. Leaving the house-boat at Kanibal, near Islamabad, we ride through a charming country, not so flat and swampy as the lower portion of the valley. We approach the semicircle of mountains which bound the valley on the east. Numerous streams rush down from the mountains. The valley is divided up into rice-fields, and is everywhere dotted over with hamlets hidden among chenar, mulberry, walnut, and pear or apple trees. Passing through one of these villages, which is alive with running water, and completely overshadowed by massive chenar trees, we enter a garden of the usual Moghal type, with a straight line of fountains and waterfalls, and an avenue of chenars. At the head of the garden is the mountain-side covered with deodar forest, and welling out of the mountain is a rushing stream of clean, clear water. It is a delicious and remarkable sight; but I think the spot would be more beautiful if the natural conditions had been preserved, and the artificial garden 117and unsightly buildings had not been constructed round it. For they only serve to hide the magnificent prospect right down the length of the Kashmir valley and the snowy mountains on either hand.

A SRINAGAR BAZAAR

It is, however, in spite of this a fascinating spot, and the camp which the Maharaja pitched here for the entertainment of Lord Minto was the prettiest I have ever seen, for the lines of the tents accorded with the formality of the garden, and the running water, the fountains, and the waterfalls gave a special charm to the encampment.

CHAPTER VII

SPORT

Sport is, as is well known, one of the chief attractions of Kashmir. Every year, like the swallows, with the coming of spring, tonga loads of ardent sportsmen begin swarming into the country. Nowadays they cannot, as formerly, shoot wherever they like and as much as they like; and in their own interests it is well they cannot, for if they still had the freedom of former days no game would now be left. For some years past a Game Preservation Department has been formed by the Maharaja, and placed under the charge of a retired British officer, that keen sportsman Major Wigram. Licences to shoot have now to be taken out, and regulations for sportsmen are published annually. Certain localities are strictly preserved for the Maharaja's own use and for the entertainment of his guests. Others are reserved for Raja Sir Amar Singh. Others 119again as sanctuaries. The number of head of the various kind of game which a sportsman may shoot is laid down. The number of sportsmen which may be permitted to visit each locality in the year is fixed. And regulations determine how the places are allotted among the numerous applicants. Major Wigram has also under him an establishment to prevent poaching by the natives, and he himself is incessantly touring and keeping a watch on the due preservation of the game. He obtains an income of about Rs. 25,000 per annum from the sale of licences, and spends about Rs. 20,000.

Under these conditions sport in Kashmir will always remain. The total bags of big game for the last two years are:—

	907	906
Ibex	19	60
Markhor	1	2
Stags	9	1
Black bears	23	26
Brown bears	2	9
Leopards	2	7
Shapoo	00	5
Burhel	4	7
Goa	7	7
Ovis ammon	6	5

These figures do not include what was shot in 120the Maharaja's preserve, but they were not all shot within the limits of the Kashmir Province. They include also what was shot in the high mountains at the back of Kashmir proper—in Ladak, Baltistan, and Astor.

In this last year it so happens that magnificent trophies were obtained. Captain Barstow shot a markhor of 61 inches, which is the largest "shot head" ever obtained, though a head measuring 63 inches was once picked up. In the Kajnag mountains, which tower over the Jhelum

River on the drive into Kashmir, one sportsman shot a markhor of 57½ inches, and several other heads of 50 were obtained last year. And as showing the pure luck which attends sport, it may be mentioned that Captain Barstow had never shot a markhor before he shot the record head.

Three good ibex heads, measuring close on 50 inches, were shot last year, and the other trophies shot were good. The reputation of Kashmir for sport is therefore being well maintained, though sportsmen have, in their own interest, to conform to more restriction than of old.

Last year the record ibex was also obtained by a well-known Kashmir sportsman, though not in Kashmir. Mr. Frank Hadow shot a 59½-inch head, but had the bad luck to lose it in a stream while having it cleaned.

In duck-shooting, too, last season was a record year. Mr. T. Kennard shot 325 duck in one day by himself. And Colonel Edwards twice shot over 200 to his own gun while shooting with others. But it would be a mistake to suppose that Mr. Kennard secured this record bag merely by good shooting, and by being placed down amidst a crowd of ducks as in a big ceremonial state shoot. Mr. Kennard is among the most scientific sportsmen who have ever visited Kashmir. I first met him twenty years ago when he built the first house-boat ever seen in Kashmir. He used then to come out to Kashmir regularly every cold weather, and spend many happy months shooting small game in the Kashmir valley, markhor and ibex in Baltistan, the Gilgit district, and Astor, and stag in the Kashmir mountains. No man had a more glorious time, when Major Wigram and the whole Game Preservation Department were still unthought of, and at a time of year when game was most easily obtained, and all the sportsmen in India were bound down to their official duties. After an interval of several years Mr. Kennard returned last year to Kashmir for yet another shoot. He set to work in a most methodical and business-like way. He studied his ground well. He found out exactly when most ducks came. He studied their habits. He spared himself no labour and neglected no detail. And he devoted the entire cold weather to this single sport.

Besides duck and goose shooting there is excellent chikore shooting on the hill-sides, and a few manaul pheasants may also be shot.

The Maharaja's preserves have for many years been under the management of that old and experienced sportsman and naturalist, Colonel Ward, to whose book, the *Sportsman's Guide to Kashmir and Ladak*, all those who want full information on shooting in Kashmir should refer.

And in addition to shooting, trout-fishing will soon be established as a further attraction to the sportsman.

Some years ago a number of keen fishermen banded together, and after some failure and much trouble, and with the assistance of the State authorities in Kashmir and of the Duke of Bedford in England, succeeded in introducing the ova of the English brown trout into the valley. Under the special charge of Mr. Frank Mitchell a hatchery has been established at Harwan, nine miles out of Srinagar, just beyond the Shalimar garden, and at the outlet of the Dachigam—a perfect trout stream—the valley of which is preserved for the Maharaja's shooting.

From these stock ponds a trout weighing twelve and a half pounds was taken on Lord Minto's visit in 1908. The Dachigam stream itself is now well stocked, and affords some excellent fishing to those who have obtained His Highness' permission. In addition aged ova and yearling trout have been sent to other streams in Kashmir—to the Achibal, Beoru, Wangat, Vishu, Kishenganga at Badwan, the Liddar at Aru and Tannin, Marwar, Erin. Yearlings have also been let out in the Burzil stream, the Gorai (on the north side of the Tragbal Pass), in the Gangarbal Lake, and in the Punch River.

It has been proved satisfactorily that when the snow-water has run off, the biggest trout will take a fly put to them at the right moment, though when the snow-water is coming down there are few flies rising and the fish do not take. A constant enemy of the trout is the poacher. English trout are, unfortunately, becoming very popular among the Kashmirs, and it is difficult to protect the fishing. The biggest trout caught so far is a nine-pounder caught in the Dachigam stream when the trout have been let out some years. In the summer of 1908 a fish weighing two and a half pounds, which must have been one of the yearlings turned out in 1906, was caught in the Vishu stream. By both Major Wigram and Mr. Frank Mitchell great attention is being paid to the development of trout-fishing.

Seeing the success which has attended the introduction of trout the Maharaja on the occasion of Lord Minto's visit ordered the importation of the ova of the huchon (*Salmo Hucho*), or so-called Danube salmon. Mr. Frank Mitchell in the spring of 1908 successfully introduced them, and about 2000 hatched out in the Harwan hatcheries. They will probably be put out in the rapids of the Jhelum River below Baramula, and as they run to some 26 lbs. in weight, and are known to be one of the most sporting as well as the largest of the Salmonidæ, they should afford another welcome attraction for the sportsman in Kashmir.

CHAPTER VIII

THE PEOPLE

Kashmir is very generally renowned for the beauty of its women and the deftness and taste of its shawl-weavers. And this reputation is, I think, well deserved. Sir Walter Lawrence indeed says that he has seen thousands of women in the villages, and cannot remember, save one or two exceptions, ever seeing a really beautiful face. But whether it is that Sir Walter was unfortunate, or that he is particularly hard to please, or that villages are not the abodes of Kashmir beauties, certain it is that the visitor, with an ordinary standard of beauty, as he passes along the river or the roads and streets, does see a great many more than one or two really beautiful women. He will often see strikingly handsome women, with clear-cut features, large dark eyes, well-marked eyebrows, and a general Jewish appearance. As to the deftness and taste of the weavers the shawls themselves are the best testimony.

The population of the whole Kashmir State is 2,905,578, and of the Kashmir Province 1,157,394. Of these 93 per cent of the Kashmir Province and 74 per cent of the whole State are Mohamedan, and the remainder chiefly Hindu. But the rulers are Hindus, and consequently the Mohamedans are as much in the shade as Hindus are in States ruled by Mohamedans. The ruling family is also alien, coming not from the valley itself, but from Jammu, on the far side of the mountain to the south.

The inhabitants were not, however, always Mohamedans. Originally they were Hindus. It was only in the fourteenth century that they were converted—mostly by force—to become Mohamedans. The present indigenous Hindus of the valley are generally known as Pundits, and Kashmir Pundits are well known over India for their acuteness and subtlety of mind, their intelligence and quick-wittedness. They prefer priestly, literary, and clerical occupation, but in the severe competition of life many have been compelled to make more use of their hands than their brains, and have had to take up agriculture, and become cooks, bakers, confectioners, tailors, and, indeed, to follow any trade except the following which, according to Lawrence, are barred to them—cobbler, potter, corn-frier, porter, boatman, carpenter, mason, or fruit-seller. It is hard for us occidentals to understand why the line should have been drawn at these apparently harmless occupations, but those of us who have lived in India know that the Hindu does fix his lines with extraordinary sharpness and rigidity, and a Kashmir Pundit would as much think of working as a boatman as an English gentleman would think of wearing a black tie at a formal dinner-party.

The Kashmir Pundits are essentially townspeople, and out of the total number about half live in the city of Srinagar. But they are also scattered sparsely through the villages, where the visitor will easily distinguish them by the caste mark on the forehead. On the whole they have a cultured look about them and a superior bearing.

The Mohamedans, forming the large majority of the population, strictly speaking having no caste, are engaged in various occupations, and found in every grade of social life. And the Mohamedan gentleman of good position has something singularly attractive about him. He combines dignity with deference to a noteworthy degree, and between him and the European there is not that gulf of caste fixed which makes such a bar to intercourse with Hindus. Not that the Mohamedans of India have not absorbed to a certain degree the atmosphere of caste with which they are surrounded. They are not so entirely free in their customs and behaviour as their co-religionists in purely Mohamedan countries. When travelling in Turkestan I lived with Mohamedans, slept in their houses and tents, ate with them, and generally consorted with them with a freedom that Mohamedans in India would think prejudicial to some vague sense of caste which, theoretically, they are not supposed to have, but which in practice they have absorbed from the atmosphere of Hinduism which they breathe. The Mohamedan, even of Kashmir, is not quite so unrestricted as the Mohamedan of Central Asia. Still, he is a very attractive gentleman, and though not easily found, for nowadays he lives in some pride of seclusion, and in the pestering importunate merchant the visitor sees but a sorry representative of the class, yet he is occasionally met with—grave, sedate, polite, and full of interesting conversation, and bearing with him a sense of former greatness when his religion was in the ascendant in the seats of power. These old-fashioned Mohamedan gentlemen have little or no English education, but they have a culture of their own; and among the mullas may be found men of great learning.

A CORNER OF THE VILLAGE OF PAHLGAM, LIDAR VALLEY

Other interesting types of Kashmir Mohamedans are found among the headmen of the picturesque little hamlets along the foot-hills. Here may be seen fine old patriarchal types, just as we picture to ourselves the Israelitish heroes of old. Some, indeed, say, though I must admit without much authority, that these Kashmiris are of the lost tribes of Israel. Only this year there died in the Punjab the founder of a curious sect, who maintained that he was both the Messiah of the Jews and the Mahdi of the Mohamedans; that Christ had never really died upon the Cross, but had been let down and had disappeared, as He had foretold, to seek that which was lost, by which He meant the lost tribes of Israel; and that He had come to Kashmir and was buried in Srinagar. It is a curious theory, and was worked out by this founder of the Quadiani sect in much detail. There resided in Kashmir some 1900 years ago a saint of the name of Yus Asaf, who preached in parables 130and used many of the same parables as Christ used, as, for instance, the parable of the sower. His tomb is in Srinagar, and the theory of this founder of the Quadiani sect is that Yus Asaf and Jesus are one and the same person.

When the people are in appearance of such a decided Jewish cast it is curious that such a theory should exist; and certainly, as I have said, there are real Biblical types to be seen everywhere in Kashmir, and especially among the upland villages. Here the Israelitish shepherd tending his flocks and herds may any day be seen.

Yet apart from this, the ordinary Kashmiri villager is not an attractive being. Like his house he is dirty, untidy, and slipshod, and both men and women wear the most unbecoming clothing, without either shape, grace, or colour. But the physique of both men and women is excellent. They are of medium height, but compared with the people of India of exceptional muscular strength. The men carry enormous loads. In the days before the cart-road was constructed, they might be seen carrying loads of apples sometimes up to and over 200 lbs. in weight; and the labour they do in the rice-fields is excessively severe.

A MOUNTAIN FARM-HOUSE

Good as is their physique, the Kashmiris are, however, 131for some quite unaccountable reason lamentably lacking in personal courage. A Kashmiri soldier is almost a contradiction in terms. There is not such a thing. They will patiently endure and suffer, but they will not fight. And they are very careful of the truth. As an American once said to me, they set such value on the truth that they very seldom use it.

Their good points are, that they are intelligent and can turn their hands to most things. They are, says Lawrence, excellent cultivators when they are working for themselves. A Kashmiri can weave good woollen cloth, make first-rate baskets, build himself a house, make his own sandals, his own ropes, and a good bargain. He is kind to his wife and children, and divorce scandals or immorality among villagers are rarely heard of.

He is not a cheery individual, like many hillmen in the Himalayas, but he seems to be fond of singing; and dirty as he, his wife, his house and all that belongs to him is, he has one redeeming touch of the æsthetic—all round the village he plants his graves with iris and narcissus. The final conclusion one has, then, is that if only he would wash, if only he would dress his wife in some brighter and cleaner clothes, and if only he would make his house stand upright, then with the good 132points he already has, and with all Nature to back him, he would make Kashmir literally perfection.

The boatmen, who are the class with whom visitors to Kashmir come most intimately into contact, are a separate tribe from the villagers. They are said to claim Noah as their ancestor, and certain it is that if they did not borrow the pattern of their boats from Noah's ark, Noah must have borrowed the pattern from them. They are known as Hanji or Manjis, and live permanently on their boats with their families complete. Some of these boats will carry between six and seven thousand pounds of grain. Others are light passenger boats. They all have their little cooking place on board, and a gigantic wooden pestle and mortar in which the women pound the rice. Both men and women have extremely fluent and sharp tongues, and have not so far earned the reputation for truthfulness. But they are quick-witted, and can turn their hands to most things, and make themselves useful in a variety of ways.

Besides carrying goods and passengers among the numerous waterways of Kashmir, some gather the singháre (water nuts) on the Wular Lake, others work market gardens on the Dal Lake, others fish, and others dredge for driftwood in the rivers.

A BOATMAN AND HIS FAMILY
CHAPTER IX

133

THE HISTORY OF KASHMIR

A country of such striking natural beauty must, surely, at some period of its history have produced a refined and noble people? Amid these glorious mountains, breathing their free and bracing air, and brightened by the constant sunshine, there must have sprung a strong virile and yet æsthetic race? The beautiful Greece, with its purple hills and varied contour, its dancing seas and clear blue sky, produced the graceful Greeks. But Kashmir is more beautiful than Greece. It has the same blue sky and brilliant sunshine, but its purple hills are on a far grander scale, and if it has no sea, it has lake and river, and the still more impressive snowy mountains. It has, too, greater variety of natural scenery, of field and forest, of rugged mountain and open valley. And to me who have seen both countries, Kashmir seems much the more likely to 134impress a race by its natural beauty. Has it ever made any such impression?

The shawls for which the country is noted are some indication that its inhabitants have a sense of form and colour, and some delicacy and refinement. But a great people would have produced something more impressive than shawls. Are there no remains of buildings, roads, aqueducts, canals, statues, or any other such mark by which a people leaves its impress on a country? And is there any literature or history?

RUINS OF TEMPLES, WANGAT, SIND VALLEY

All over the Kashmir valley there are remains of temples remarkable for their almost Egyptian solidity, simplicity, and durability, as well as for what Cunningham describes as the graceful elegance of their outlines, the massive boldness of their parts, and the happy propriety of their outlines. The ancient Kashmirian architecture, with its noble fluted pillars, its vast colonnades, its lofty pediments, and its elegant trefoiled arches, is, he thinks, entitled to be classed as a distinct style; and we may take it as implying the existence of just such a people as this mountain country might be expected to produce. Three miles beyond Uri, on the road into Kashmir, are the ruins of a temple of extremely pleasing execution. Near Buniar, 135just beyond Rampur, is another right on the road. At Patan, 13 miles before reaching Srinagar, are two more ruined temples of massive construction. Two and a half miles southward of Shadipur, the present junction of the Sind River with the Jhelum, are the remains of a town, the extent and nature of which show conclusively that it must once have been a large and important centre. On the summit of the hill, rising above the European quarter in Srinagar, is a dome-shaped temple erroneously known as the Takht-i-Suliman. At Pandrathan, three miles from Srinagar, is a graceful little temple and the remains of a statue of Buddha, and of a column of immense strength and size. At Pampur and Avantipur, on the road to Islamabad at Payech, on the southern side of the valley, where there is the best preserved specimen temple, and at many other places in the main valley, and in the Sind and Lidar valleys, there are remains of temples of much the same style. But it is at Martand that there is the finest, and as it is not only typical of Kashmir architecture at its best, but is built on the most sublime site occupied by any building in the world,—finer far than the site of the Parthenon, or of the Taj, or of St. Peters, or of the Escurial,—we 136may take it as the representative, or rather the culmination of all the rest, and by it we must judge the people of Kashmir at their best.

On a perfectly open and even plain, gently sloping away from a background of snowy mountains, looking directly out on the entire length both of the smiling Kashmir valley and of the snowy ranges which bound it—so situated, in fact, as to be encircled by, yet not overwhelmed by, snowy mountains—stand the ruins of a temple second only to the Egyptians in massiveness and strength, and to the Greek in elegance and grace. It is built of immense rectilinear blocks of limestone, betokening strength and durability. Its outline and its detail are bold, simple, and impressive. And any over-weighing sense of massiveness is relieved by the elegance of the surrounding colonnade of graceful Greek-like pillars. It is but a ruin now, but yet, with the other ruins so numerous in the valley, and so similar in their main characteristics, it denotes the former presence in Kashmir of a people worthy of study. No one without an eye for natural beauty would have chosen that special site for the construction of a temple, and no one with an inclination to the ephemeral and transient would have built it on 137so massive and enduring a scale. We cannot, for instance, imagine present-day Kashmiris building anything so noble, so simple, so true, and so enduring. The people that built the ancient temples of Kashmir must have been religious, for the remains are all of temples or of sacred emblems, and not of palaces, commercial offices, or hotels; they must have held, at least, one large idea to have built on so enduring a scale, and they must have been men of strong and simple tastes, averse to the paltry and the florid. What was their history? Were they a purely indigenous race? Were they foreigners and conquerors settled in the land, or were they a native race, much influenced from outside, and with sufficient pliability to assimilate that influence and turn it to profitable use for their own ends?

RUINED GATEWAY OF MARTAND

Fortunately one of their native historians has left us a record, and Dr. Stein's skill and industry in translating and annotating this record makes it possible to obtain a fairly clear idea of ancient Kashmir. From this and from the style of the ruins themselves, we gather that the main impulses came from outside rather than from within, from India and from Greece. And perhaps, if in place of their mountains, which tend to seclusion and 138cut a people off from the full effects of that important factor in the development of a race, easy intercourse and strenuous rivalry with other peoples, the Kashmirians had, like the Greeks, been in contact with the sea, with ready access to other peoples and other civilisations, they might have made a greater mark in the world's history. But they had this advantage, that the beauty of their country must always, as now, in itself have been an attraction to outsiders, and so from the very commencement of its authentic history we find strong outside influences at work in the country.

Thus among the first authentic facts we can safely lay hold of from among the misty and elusive statements of exuberant Oriental historians, is the fact that Asoka's sovereign power extended to Kashmir-Asoka, the contemporary of Hannibal, and the enthusiastic Buddhist ruler of India, whose kingdom extended from Bengal to the Deccan, to Afghanistan and to the Punjab, and the results of whose influence may be seen to this day in Kashmir, in the remains of Buddhist temples and statues, and in the ruins of cities founded by him 250 years before Christ, 200 years before 139the Romans landed in Britain, and 700 years before what is now known as England had yet been trodden by truly English feet.

RUINED TEMPLES OF AVANTIPUR

At this time Buddhism was the dominating religion in northern India, and perhaps received an additional impulse from the Greek kingdoms in the Punjab, planted by Alexander the Great as the result of his invasion in 327 B.C. Asoka had organised it on the basis of a state religion, he had spread the religion with immense enthusiasm, and in Kashmir he caused stupas and temples to be erected, and founded the original city of Srinagar, then situated on the site of the present village of Pandrathan, three miles above the existing capital. He had broken through the fetters of Brahminism and established a friendly intercourse with Greece and Egypt, and it is to this connection that the introduction of stone architecture and sculpture is due. The Punjab contains examples of Græco-Buddhist art, and Kashmir history dawns at the time when Greek influence was most prominent in India.

The first great impulse which has left its mark on the ages came, then, not from within, but from without—not from within Kashmir, but from India, Greece, and Egypt. Little, indeed, now 140remains of that initial movement. The religion which was its mainspring has now not a single votary among the inhabitants of the valley. The city Asoka founded has long since disappeared. But the great record remains; and on a site beautiful even for Kashmir, where the river sweeps gracefully round to kiss the spur on which the city was built, and from whose sloping terraces the inhabitants could look out over the smiling fields, the purple hills, and snowy mountain summits of their lovely country, there still exist the remnants of the ancient glory as the last, but everlasting sign that once great men ruled the land.

The next great landmark in Kashmir history is the reign of the king Kanishka, the Indo-Scythian ruler of upper India. He reigned about 40A.D., when the Romans were conquering Britain and Buddhism was just beginning to spread to China. He was of Turki descent, and was part of that wave of Scythian immigration which for two or three hundred years came pouring down from Central Asia. And he was renowned throughout the Buddhist world as the pious Buddhist king, who held in Kashmir the famous Third Great Council of the Church which drew up the 141Northern Canon or "Greater Vehicle of the Law." In his time, too, there lived at a site which is still traceable at Harwan, nestling under the higher mountains at the entrance of one of the attractive side-valleys of Kashmir, and overlooking the placid waters of the Dal Lake, a famous Bodhisattva, Nagarjuna, who from this peaceful retreat exercised a spiritual lordship over the land.

Buddhism was, in fact, at the zenith of its power in Kashmir. But a reaction against it was soon to follow, and from this time onward the orthodox Brahministic Hinduism, from which Buddhism was a revolt, reasserted itself, and Buddhism steadily waned. When the Chinese Buddhist pilgrim Hiuen Tsiang visited Kashmir, about A.D. 631, he said, "This kingdom is not much given to the faith, and the temples of the heretics are their sole thought."

Passing now over a period of six centuries, the only authentically recorded event in which is the reign, A.D. 515, of Mihirakula, the "White Hun," a persecutor of the Buddhist faith, "a man of violent acts and resembling Death," whose approach the people knew "by noticing the vultures, crows, and other birds which were flying ahead eager to feed on those who were to be slain," and who 142succeeded to a kingdom which extended to Kabul and Central India, we come to the reign of the most famous king in Kashmir history, and the first really indigenous ruler of note—Lalitaditya. And of his reign we must take especial notice as Kashmir was then at its best.

Whether Lalitaditya was a pure Kashmiri it is impossible to discover. His grandfather, the founder of the dynasty to which he belonged, was a man of humble origin—whether Kashmiri or foreign the historian does not relate—who was connected by marriage with the preceding ruling family. His mother was the mistress of a merchant settled in Srinagar. The dynasty which his grandfather succeeded was foreign, and it is impossible, therefore, to say how much foreign blood Lalitaditya had in his veins; but his family had at any rate been settled in Kashmir for a couple of generations, and Kashmir was not in his time the mere appanage of a greater kingdom, but was a distinct and isolated kingdom in itself. From this time for many centuries onwards, till the time of Akbar, the tide of conquest and political influence was to turn, and instead of more advanced and masterful races from the direction of India spreading their influence [143]over Kashmir, it was from Kashmir that conquerors were to go forth to extend their sway over neighbouring districts in the Punjab.

Lalitaditya's reign extended from about 699 to 736. He was therefore a contemporary of Charlemagne, and preceded our own King Alfred by more than a century. Mohamed was already dead a hundred years, but his religion had not yet spread to India. The Kashmiri historians speak of Lalitaditya's "conquering the world," and mix up much fable with fact. But what certainly is true is that he asserted his authority over the hilly tracts of the northern Punjab, that he attacked and reduced the King of Kanauj to submission, that he conquered the Tibetans, successfully invaded Badakhshan in Central Asia, and sent embassies to Peking.

Though, then, he was not the "universal 'monarch' that the historian described him, and did not move round the earth like the sun," or "putting his foot on the islands as if they were stepping-stones, move quickly and without difficulty over the ocean," he is yet the most conspicuous figure in Kashmir history, and raised his country to a pitch of glory it had never reached before or attained to since. It was he who erected the temple at [144]Martand; and the ruins of the city Parihasapura, near the present Shadipur, are an even fuller testimony to his greatness. These, therefore, we must regard as the most reliable indication we have of the degree of culture and civilisation to which Kashmir attained in its most palmy day twelve hundred years ago.

Lalitaditya's rule was followed by a succession of short and weak reigns, but his grandson was almost as great a hero of popular legend as himself. He too, "full of ambition, collected an army and set out for the conquest of the world." He reached the Ganges and defeated the King of Kanauj, but had to return to Kashmir to subdue a usurper to his throne. He encouraged scholars and poets and founded cities. After him followed, first, "an indolent and profligate prince"; then a child in the hands of uncles, who as soon as he grew up destroyed him and put another child on the throne. He indeed maintained his position on the throne for 37 years, but only on account of the rivalries of the uncles, and as a mere puppet king, and was eventually deposed by the victorious faction to make place for yet another puppet king, who again was killed by a treacherous relative. So the [145]record goes on till we come to the reign of Avantivarman, 855-883, and this appears to have brought a period of consolidation for the country, which must have greatly suffered economically as well as politically from the internal troubles during the preceding reigns. There is no indication of the reassertion of Kashmir sovereignty abroad, but there is ample proof of the internal recovery of the country, and the town of Avantipura, named after the king, has survived to the present day. It lies one march above Srinagar, and the ruins of the ancient buildings, though not equal in size to Lalitaditya's structures, yet rank, says Stein, among the most imposing monuments of ancient Kashmir architecture, and sufficiently attest the resources of the builder.

This reign was, too, remarkable for the execution of an engineering scheme to prevent floods and drain the valley, a precisely similar idea to that on which Major de Lotbinière is working under the direction of the present Maharaja. The Kashmiri engineer Suyya, after whom is named the present town of Sopur, saw more than a thousand years ago what modern engineers have also observed, that floods in the valley are due to the waters of the Jhelum not being able to get through the gorge [146]three miles below Baramula with sufficient rapidity. The constricted passage gets blocked with boulders, and both Suyya and our present engineers saw that this obstruction must be removed. But while Major de Lotbinière imported electrically-worked dredgers from America and a dredging engineer from Canada, Suyya adopted a much simpler method: he threw money into the river where the obstruction lay. His contemporaries, as perhaps we also would have, looked upon him as a madman. But there was method in his madness, for the report had no sooner got about that there was money at the bottom of the river than men dashed in to find it, and rooted up all the obstructing boulders in their search. So at least says the legend. In any case the obstruction was removed by Suyya, and the result was the regulation of the course of the river, a large increase of land available for cultivation, and increased protection against disastrous floods. May the modern Suyya be equally successful!

The successor of Avantivarman, after defeating a cousin and other rivals to the throne, started on a round of foreign expedition, in the historian's words, "to revive the tradition of the conquest of the world." The practical result does not appear to [147]have been much more than an invasion of Hazara, an attack on Kangra and the subjugation of what is now the town of Gujrat in the Punjab, since remarkable as the spot where we finally overthrew the power of the Sikhs. But the record is of interest, as showing that the conquering tendency was still from Kashmir outwards, and not from the Punjab into Kashmir.

But this was the last outward effort, and from this reign onward the record is one long succession of struggles between the rulers and usurping uncles, cousins, brothers, ministers, nobles, and soldiers. The immediate successor was a child whose regent mother was under the influence of her paramour the Minister. After two years he was murdered by the Minister. Another boy succeeded who only lived ten days. Then the regent mother herself ruled for a couple of years, but a military faction overruled her councils, and by open rebellion obtained the throne for a nominee of their own, and the land became oppressed by exactions of the soldiery backed by unscrupulous ministers. The Queen was captured and executed, and a disastrous flood and terrible famine increased the general misery. After two years' reign the soldiers' nominee was deposed and a child put in his place. Then there was a fresh revolution and still another nominee, who, as he could not pay a sufficient bribe to the soldiery, was deposed and the crown sold to the Minister.

And now another power makes itself felt, the influence of the feudal landholders, whose interests had suffered from the prolonged predominance of the military party. They marched upon Srinagar, defeated the soldiers, threw out the usurping minister, and restored the legitimate king, who, however, showed little gratitude, but abandoned himself to vile cruelties and excesses, till the feudal landholders became so exasperated that they treacherously murdered him at night within the arms of one of his low-caste queens. The successor was no better. He surpassed his predecessor in acts of senseless cruelty and wanton licence, and was encouraged by his ambitious minister (who was scheming to secure the throne for himself) to destroy his own relatives. Some were murdered, and others captured and allowed to starve to death. He himself died after a reign of only two years, and his successor had to flee after occupying the throne for a few days. The commander-in-chief tried to seize it, but on placing the election in the hands of an assembly of Brahmins, they chose one of their own number, who for nine years, by a wise and mild rule, gained a respite from the constant troubles of previous reigns. Only a short respite, however, for on his death the aforementioned scheming minister, after first putting his rivals out of the way, forced an entrance to the palace, killed the successor of the Brahmin, and threw him into the Jhelum. He grossly oppressed the land for a year and a half, and then died of dropsy, to be succeeded by a youth grossly sensual and addicted to many vices, who married a princess of the house of Punch. This lady happened to have considerable force of character, and when her son succeeded as a child, exercised as his guardian full royal power. She ruthlessly put down all rival parties, executing captured rebels, exterminating their families. She even, on her son's death, murdered two of her own grandsons that she might herself retain power. Finally, she fell in love with a letter-carrier who had begun life as a herdsman; she appointed him her Minister, and he retained undisputed predominance over her for her reign of twenty-three years, his valour supplementing her cunning diplomacy and bribes in overcoming all opposition.

The following reign, which was prudent, but weak, is noticeable from the fact that the famous Mahmud of Ghazni, who forced Mohamedanism upon upper India, made an attempt, A.D. 1015, to invade Kashmir. It was unsuccessful, but it marks the first sign of the returning flood of invasion from the Punjab inwards to Kashmir. The outward flow had ceased. The inward was now to begin.

In the meanwhile, until the Moghals, five hundred years later, finally established themselves in Kashmir, the ceaseless round of intrigue, treachery, and strife continued. The powerful herdsman minister and his son were foully murdered, and a succession of low favourites rose to power and plundered the people. A reign of twenty-two days which follows was terminated by the licentious mother killing her own son. Then comes a dangerous rising of the feudal landholders and more short reigns, murders, suicides, till we arrive at the reign of Harsa, 1089-1101, who is said to have been "the most striking figure among the later Hindu rulers of Kashmir." He was courageous and fond of display, and well versed in various sciences, and a lover of music and the arts, but "cruelty and kindheartedness, liberality and greed, violent self-willedness and reckless supineness, cunning and want of thought, in turn displayed themselves in his chequered life." He kept up a splendid Court and was munificent to men of learning and poets. He also succeeded in asserting his authority in the hilly country outside Kashmir on the south. But he eventually became the object of conspiracies, and to put them down resorted to the cruellest measures. He had his half-brother, as well as his nephews, and some other relatives, who had given no cause for suspicion, heartlessly murdered. Extravagant expenditure on the troops and senseless indulgence in costly pleasures gradually involved Harsa in grave financial trouble, from which he endeavoured to free himself by ruthless spoliation of sacred shrines, and even by confiscating divine images made of any valuable metal. He was further reduced to the necessity of imposing new and oppressive imposts. All this misgovernment spread discontent and misery among the people; and while the plague was raging, and robbers everywhere infesting the land, there occurred a disastrous flood which brought on a famine. A rising against Harsa was the result. He was slain in the fighting; his head was cut off and burned, while his body, naked like that of a pauper, was cremated by a compassionate wood-dealer.152

The position of his successor, Vecula, was no less precarious than that of the generality of Kashmir rulers. His younger brother was ready to rise against him, and the leaders of feudal landholders, to whose rebellion he owed his throne, behaved as the true rulers of the land. He protected himself by fomenting jealousy and mutual suspicion, and murdered or exiled their most influential leaders, and then openly turned upon the remainder and forced them to disarm and submit. He also systematically persecuted the officials. On the other hand he showed considerate regard for the common people, and was on the whole a liberal, capable, and fairly energetic ruler. Nevertheless he, too, met with a violent end. The city-prefect and his brothers attacked him at night in the palace as, unarmed and attended only by a few followers, he was proceeding to the seraglio. He fought with desperate bravery, but was soon overpowered by his numerous assailants and cruelly murdered, December 1111.

His immediate successor reigned only a few hours; his half-brother only four months. He was then made prisoner by his brother, whose reign of eight years was one succession of internal troubles caused by rebellious and powerful landholders 153whom he in vain tried to subdue. He imprisoned his Minister and the Minister's three sons, and finally had them all strangled. He executed with revolting cruelty some hostages of the landholders; and, finally, in face of a rebellion caused by his cruelty and by his oppressive imposts, he had to fly from Srinagar to Punch. A pretender occupied the throne for a year, during which the people were at the mercy of bands of rebels, while rival ministers contended for what was left of regal power. Trade was at a standstill and money scarce. The rightful ruler returned and again occupied the throne, and, owing to the want of union among the feudal landholders, was able to retain it for another five years. But eventually he also met the usual fate of Kashmir kings, and was murdered.

Jayashima, the successor, reigned for twenty-one years, though he had found his country in a pitiable state. The feudal landholders were like kings, while the resources of the King and people alike were well-nigh exhausted by the preceding struggles. His predecessor had been unable by force to permanently reduce the power and pretensions of these petty nobles, and Jayashima tried to effect the same object by cunning diplomacy 154and unscrupulous intrigue. But he was no more successful, and they continued to preserve a rebellious, independent attitude for centuries later, far into the Mohamedan period.

The accounts of this and the immediately preceding reigns are of particular interest, because Kalhana, the historian to whom the facts are due, lived at this period. We get then a first-hand account of the state of Kashmir eight hundred years ago. It is a petty, melancholy, and sordid history, but it is the record of a contemporary, and I have no hesitation in adopting it as giving a true impression of the state of the country, because I have myself seen a precise counterpart of it in independent states on this very frontier. When I visited Hunza in 1889 the then chief—now in exile—had murdered his father, poisoned his mother, and thrown his two brothers over a precipice. The chief of Chitral, when I was there in 1893, was one of only four survivors of seventeen brothers who were living when their father died, and he himself was subsequently murdered by one of his three surviving brothers—a brother whom he had frequently asked my permission to murder, on the ground that if he did not murder the brother, the 155brother would murder him. In Chitral there was also the same struggle with "nobles" as is recorded of Kashmir, and murders of "nobles" were horribly frequent.

We may accept, then, as authentic that the normal state of Kashmir for many centuries, except in the intervals when a strong, firm ruler came to the front, was a state of perpetual intrigue and assassination, of struggles with brothers, cousins, uncles, before a chief even came to the throne; of fights for power with ministers, with the military, with the "nobles" when he was on it; of constant fear; of poisoning and assassination; of wearying, petty internecine "wars," and of general discomfort, uncertainty, and unrest.

For two centuries more Hindu rule maintained itself, but it was steadily decaying. In the meanwhile Mohamedanism had, especially in consequence of the invasion of Mahmud of Ghazni in 1000 A.D., made great advances in the adjoining kingdoms of the Punjab; and, in 1339, a Mohamedan ruler, Shah Mir, deposed the widow of the last Hindu ruler and founded a Mohamedan dynasty. The influx of foreign adventurers from Central Asia as well as from India had prepared 156the ground for Mohamedan rule, and when Shah Mir appeared there was little change in the system of administration, which remained as before in the hands of the traditional official class, the Brahmins.

From this time till the Moghal emperors finally conquered Kashmir in 1586, there was, with one exception, the usual succession of weak rulers and constant struggles between rival factions of territorial magnates. But this one exception is worthy of notice, as his reign is even now quoted by Kashmiris as the happiest of their history. Zain-ul-ab-ul-din (1420-70) was virtuous in his private life and liberal. He was the staunch friend of the cultivators, and built many bridges and constructed many canals. He was fond of sport, and was tolerant towards Brahmins, remitting the poll-tax on them, and encouraging them by grants of land. He also repaired some Hindu temples and revived Hindu learning. Further, he introduced many art-manufactures from foreign countries, and his Court was thronged by poets, musicians, and singers.

GATE OF THE OUTER WALL, HARI PARBAT FORT, SRINAGAR

But this reign seems to have been a mere oasis in the dreary record, and it was followed by a succession of weak reigns till 1532, when a direct conquest of the country by a foreign invader was effected. In that year Mirza Haider, with a following 157which formed part of the last great wave of Turkis (or Moghals) from the north, invaded Kashmir and held it for some years. Then followed one last short period, during which Kashmir became once more the scene of long-continued strife among the great feudal families, who set up and deposed their puppet kings in rapid succession, till finally, in 1586, Kashmir was incorporated in the dominions of the great Akbar, the contemporary of Elizabeth, and remained as a dependency of the Moghal emperors for nearly two centuries.

Akbar himself visited the country three times, made a land revenue settlement, and built the fort of Hari Parbat, which from its situation on an isolated hill, in a flat valley surrounded by mountains, bears some resemblance to the Potala at Lhasa. Akbar's successor, Jehangir, was devoted to Kashmir and he it was who built the stately pleasure gardens, the Shalimar and Nishat Baghs, where we can imagine that he and his wife, the famous Nurmahal, for whom he built the Taj at Agra, must have spent many a pleasant summer day.

The rule of the Moghals was fairly just and enlightened, and their laws and ordinances were 158excellent in spirit. Bernier, who visited Kashmir in the train of Aurungzebe, makes no allusion, as travellers of a subsequent date so frequently do, to the misery of the people, but, on the contrary, says of them that they are "celebrated for wit, and considered much more intelligent and ingenious than the Indians." "In poetry and the sciences," he continues, "they are not inferior to the Persians, and they are also very active and industrious." And he notes the "prodigious quantity of shawls which they manufacture." Kashmir was indeed, according to Bernier, "the terrestrial paradise of the Indies." "The whole kingdom wears the appearance," he says, "of a fertile and highly cultivated garden. Villages and hamlets are frequently seen through the luxuriant foliage. Meadows and vineyards, fields of rice, wheat, hemp, saffron, and many sorts of vegetables, among which are mingled trenches filled with water, rivulets, canals, and several small lakes, vary the enchanting scene. The whole ground is enamelled with our European flowers and plants, and covered with our apple, pear, plum, apricot, and walnut trees, all bearing fruit in great abundance."

All this and the absence of remarks on ruined towns and deserted villages, such as we shall hear so 159much of later on, implies prosperity. And of the governors of Kashmir under the Moghals, we read that many were enlightened, reduced taxation, and put down the oppression of petty officials. But as the Moghal Empire began to decay, the governors became more independent and high-handed. The Hindus were more oppressed. The officials fought among themselves, and Kashmir fell once more into wild disorder; and eventually, in 1750, came under the cruellest and worst rule of all—the rule of the Afghans, who to this day are of all the oppressive rulers in the world the most tyrannical. The period of Afghan rule was, says Lawrence, a time of "brutal tyranny, unrelieved by good works, chivalry, or honour." Men with interest were appointed as governors, who wrung as much money as they could out of the wretched people of the valley. It was said of them that they thought no more of cutting off heads than of plucking a flower. One used to tie up the Hindus, two and two, in grass sacks and sink them in the Dal Lake. The poll-tax on Hindus was revived, and many either fled the country, were killed, or converted to Islam.

At last the oppression became so unendurable that the Kashmiris turned with hope to Ranjit 160Singh, the powerful Sikh ruler of the Punjab, who, after an unsuccessful attempt, finally in 1819, accompanied by Raja Gulab Singh of Jammu, defeated the Afghan governor and annexed Kashmir to his dominions. It came then once again under Hindu rulers, though in the meantime nine-tenths of the population had been converted to Mohamedanism.

But the unfortunate country had still to suffer many ills. The Sikhs who succeeded the Afghans were not so barbarically cruel, but they were hard and rough masters. Moorcroft, who visited the country in 1824, says that "everywhere the people were in the most abject condition, exorbitantly taxed by the Sikh Government, and subjected to every kind of extortion and oppression by its officers ... not one-sixteenth of the cultivable surface is in cultivation, and the inhabitants, starving at home, are driven in great numbers to the plains of Hindustan." The cultivators were "in a condition of extreme wretchedness," and the Government, instead of taking only one-half of the produce on the threshing-floor, had now advanced its demands to three-quarters. Every shawl was taxed 26 per cent upon the estimated value, besides which there was an import duty on the 161wool with which they were manufactured, and a charge was made upon every shop or workman connected with the manufacture. Every trade was also taxed, "butchers, bakers, boatmen, vendors of fuel, public notaries, scavengers, prostitutes, all paid a sort of corporation tax, and even the Kotwal, or chief officer of justice, paid a large gratuity of thirty thousand rupees a year for his appointment, being left to reimburse himself as he might."

AT THE RIVER'S EDGE, SRINAGAR

Villages, where Moorcroft stopped in the Lolab direction, were half-deserted, and the few inhabitants that remained wore the semblance of extreme wretchedness. Islamabad was "as filthy a place as can well be imagined, and swarming with beggars." Shupaiyon was not half-inhabited, and the inhabitants of the country round, "half-naked and miserably emaciated, presented a ghastly picture of poverty and starvation." The Sikhs "seemed to look upon the Kashmirians as little better than cattle ... the murder of a native by a Sikh is punished by a fine to the Government of from sixteen to twenty rupees, of which four rupees are paid to the family of the deceased if a Hindu, and two rupees if a Mohamedan."

Vigne's description is hardly more favourable. 162He visited Kashmir in 1835. Shupaiyon was "a miserable place, bearing the impression of once having been a thriving town. The houses were in ruins." Islamabad was "but a shadow of its former self." The houses "present a ruined and neglected appearance, in wretched contrast with their once gay and happy condition, and speak volumes upon the light and joyous prosperity that has long fled the country on account of the shameless rapacity of the ruthless Sikhs." The villages were fallen into decay. The rice-ground was uncultivated for want of labour and irrigation.

Clearly the Kashmiris had not yet come to a haven of rest, but they were nearing it.

The Raja Gulab Singh of Jammu has already been mentioned as accompanying Ranjit Singh's troops on their victorious march to Kashmir in 1819. On the death of Ranjit Singh there was much violence and mutiny among the Sikh soldiery, and the Governor of Kashmir was murdered by them. Thereupon a body of about 5000 men, nominally under the command of the son of Sher Singh, Ranjit's successor, but really under the charge of Gulab Singh, was sent to Kashmir to restore authority. This was in the year 1841, 163when the British were still behind the Sutlej, but were engaged in the fruitless and disastrous expedition to Kabul, which resulted in the murder of the envoy. Gulab Singh quelled the mutiny in Kashmir, placed there a governor of his own, and from this time he became virtual master of the valley, though till the year 1846 it nominally belonged to the Sikh rulers at Lahore.

LALLA ROOKH'S TOMB, HASSAN ABDA

As he was the founder of the present ruling dynasty, it will be well to pause here to describe who he was and where he came from. He was what is known as a Dogra Rajput, that is, a Rajput inhabiting the Dogra country—the hilly country stretching down to the plains of the Punjab from the snowy range bounding Kashmir on the south. His far-away ancestors were Rajputs who for generations had followed warlike operations. Originally settled in Oudh or in Rajputana they eventually moved to the Punjab, and settled at Mirpur in the Dogra country. One branch then migrated to Chamba, another to Kangra, and the one to which Gulab Singh belonged to Jammu, where the great-great-grand-uncle of Gulab Singh—Throv Deo—was during the middle of the eighteenth century a man of importance. In 1775 the son of Throv Deo built the palace at Jammu, 164and about 1788 Gulab Singh was born. In 1807, when Ranjit Singh's troops were attacking Jammu, Gulab Singh so distinguished himself that he gained the favour of Ranjit Singh. He took service under the Sikh ruler, and with the assistance of his brother, Ranjit Singh's Dewan, acquired such influence that when the principality of Jammu had been annexed by the Sikhs, Ranjit Singh in 1818 conferred it upon Gulab Singh, with the title of Raja. The brother, Dhyan Singh, was likewise made Raja of Punch, and the third brother, Raja of Ramnager.

In the course of the next 15 years the three brothers subdued all the neighbouring principalities, and Gulab Singh's troops under Zorawar Singh had conquered Ladak and Baltistan, and even invaded Tibet, though there Zorawar Singh himself was killed and his army annihilated.

Thus when Ranjit Singh died in 1839 Gulab Singh, though still feudatory to the Sikh Government, had established his authority in Jammu and neighbouring principalities, and in Ladak and Baltistan, and he had a commanding influence in Kashmir then still under a Sikh governor. The traveller Vigne saw him in this year at Jammu, and speaks of him as feared for his cruelty and 165tyrannical exactions—very common and, it would almost appear, *necessary* characteristics of strong rulers in those unruly times—but he remarks on his tolerance and liberality in religious matters. He was never a popular ruler, and the people feared and dreaded him; but he had courage and energy, and above all was successful.

BRIDGE OF BURBUR SHAH, CHENAR BAGH, SRINAGAR

On Ranjit Singh's death all was once more in the melting-pot, and for a time it looked as if Gulab Singh would come crashing down even faster than he had risen. His influence at the Lahore Court was lost through the murder of his brother. He himself was attacked by the Sikhs and taken to Lahore. His fortunes were sinking rapidly. Then suddenly there was a turn in the wheel of fortune; and the man who had started life as a courtier of Ranjit Singh, was confirmed in the possession not only of all that he had subsequently acquired by his own prowess, but also of the rich and beautiful vale of Kashmir as well. On the payment of three-quarters of a million sterling down, and of an annual tribute of one horse, twelve goats, and six pairs of shawls, all this was confirmed by the strongest power in Asia to himself and his heirs for ever. It was one 166of those wonderful strokes of fortune which must have lent such zest and interest to life in those otherwise sordid days.

It was due to the advent of the British upon the scene. On the death of the strong, stern ruler, Ranjit Singh, the Punjab had fallen into a state of hopeless anarchy. His successor died prematurely of excess, and Ranjit's reputed son, Sher Singh, once Governor of Kashmir, had marched upon Lahore and seized the government in 1841. The Punjab was now entirely in the hands of the Sikh soldiery, whose movements were regulated not by the will of the sovereign or of the minister, but by the dictation of army committees. The minister, Dhyan Singh (Gulab Singh's younger brother) shot the ruler Sher Singh, and was in turn murdered by a Sikh chieftain, Ajit Singh, who, again, was murdered by the Sikh soldiers. Dhulip Singh, so well known afterwards as an exile in England, and then a child of five years of age, was put on the throne, and from this time the army became the absolute master of the State, though Hira Singh, Dhyan Singh's son, and therefore nephew of Gulab Singh, was nominally minister. He tried to curb the army by distributing the regiments, but the army committees would not 167allow a single corps to leave the capital without their permission. He had eventually to flee, but he was overtaken and killed, and his head brought back in triumph to Lahore.

SPRING FLOODS IN THE KUTICAL CANAL, SRINAGAR

On Hira Singh's death the power fell into the hands of the brother of the infant Dhulip Singh's mother and her paramour, Lal Singh, a Brahmin. They increased the pay of the soldiers, and in order to keep them quiet turned them against Gulab Singh at Jammu. He was brought to Lahore and had to pay a crore (ten millions) of rupees. They were then turned against Multan. Another son of Ranjit Singh raised a revolt, but was suppressed and murdered by the regnant maternal uncle of the infant Dhulip Singh. Then this uncle was himself murdered. The mother, with the aid of the minister Lal Singh, and of Tej Singh, the commander-in-chief of the army, assumed the government and, as it is thought, with the object of employing the army, which was a positive danger to the throne, ordered an advance upon British territory. In November 1845 the Sikh army of 60,000 men with 150 guns crossed the river Sutlej which was then our frontier, and by the 16th of December was encamped by Ferozepore fort held by only 10,000 British and British Indian 168troops. A bloody and indecisive battle was fought at Mudki, December 18, 1845. Another most hard-won battle—"the most severe and critical the British army had ever fought in India"—and in which the Governor-General, Lord Hardinge, himself took part, and lost five aides-de-camp killed, and four wounded, was fought at Ferozeshah on December 21. This just stemmed the tide of invasion, but at such a cost of men and ammunition, that the British could not follow up their success till January 28, 1846, when the decisive battle of Aliwal was fought, which utterly disheartened the Government at Lahore. Lal Singh, the minister, was deposed for his incapacity, and Gulab Singh was invited from Jammu to negotiate with the Governor-General.

Here was the wonderful turn in the wheel of fortune, which, when his own brother and so many of the leading men of the Punjab had been murdered or debased, brought him alone and his descendants after him to a position of security.

LOOKING DOWN THE GURAIS VALLEY, FROM DUDHGAI VILLAGE

Gulab Singh immediately made overtures to the British Government, but the Sikh army was not yet thoroughly defeated, and it was not till after the battle of Sobraon, on February 10th, that the way for negotiations was really clear. The British troops occupied Lahore. The Sikh Government submitted, and the treaty of Lahore was concluded on March 9th. By this, amongst other things, the Sikhs ceded to the British all the hill country between the rivers Beas and Indus, "including the provinces of Kashmir and Hazara"; and "in consideration of the services rendered by Raja Golab Singh, of Jummu, to the Lahore State, towards procuring the restoration of the relations of amity between the Lahore and British Governments," the British agreed to recognise "the independent sovereignty of Raja Golab Singh in such territories and districts in the hills as may be made over to the said Raja Golab Singh, by separate agreement between himself and the British Government, with the dependencies thereof, which may have been in the Raja's possession since the time of the late Maharaja Khurruk Singh"; further, the British Government, "in consideration of the good conduct of Raja Golab Singh," agreed "to recognise his independence in such territories, and to admit him to the privileges of a separate treaty with the British Government."

A week later, on 16th March 1846, was signed this separate treaty with Gulab Singh, by which the British Government "transferred and made over, for ever, in independent possession, to Maharaja Golab Singh and the heirs male of his body, all the hilly and mountainous country, with its dependencies, situated to the eastward of the river Indus and westward of the river Ravi, including Chamba and excluding Lahoul, being part of the territories ceded to the British Government by the Lahore State." In consideration of this transfer Golab Singh was to pay the British Government 75 lakhs of rupees, and in token of the supremacy of the British Government, was "to present annually to the British Government one horse, twelve perfect shawl-goats of approved breed (six male and six female), and three pairs of Kashmir shawls." He further engaged "to join with the whole of his military force the British troops when employed within the hills, or in the territories adjoining his possessions"; and on their part the British Government engaged to "give its aid to Maharaja Golab Singh in protecting his territories from external enemies."

Thus it was that Kashmir came under its present rulers; and surprise has often been expressed that when this lovely land had actually been ceded us, after a hard and strenuous campaign, we should ever have parted with it for the paltry sum of three-quarters of a million sterling. The reasons are to be found in a letter from Sir Henry Hardinge to the Queen, published in *The Letters of Queen Victoria*. The Governor-General, writing from the neighbourhood of Lahore on 18th of February 1846—that is nearly three weeks before the treaty of Lahore was actually signed—says it appeared to him desirable "to weaken the Sikh State, which has proved itself too strong—and to show to all Asia that although the British Government has not deemed it expedient to annex this immense country of the Punjab, making the Indus the British boundary, it has punished the treachery and violence of the Sikh nation, and exhibited its powers in a manner which cannot be misunderstood." "For the same political and military reason," Sir Henry Hardinge continues, "the Governor-General hopes to be able before the negotiations are closed to make arrangements by which Cashmere may be added to the possessions of Golab Singh, declaring the Rajput Hill States with Cashmere independent of the Sikhs of the Plains." "There are difficulties in the way of this arrangement," he adds, "but considering the military power which the Sikh nation had exhibited of bringing into the field 80,000 men and 300 pieces of field artillery, it appears to the Governor-General most politic to diminish the means of this warlike people to repeat a similar aggression."

This was the reason we did not annex Kashmir. We had not yet annexed the Punjab. We did not finally conquer it till three years later, when the continued unruliness of the Sikhs and the murder of British officers had rendered a second campaign necessary. In 1846 the East India Company had no thoughts or inclinations whatever to extend their possessions. All they wished was to curb their powerful and aggressive neighbours, and they thought they would best do this, and at the same time reward a man who had shown his favourable disposition towards them, by depriving the Sikhs of the hilly country, and by handing it over to a ruler of a different race.

So Gulab Singh became nominal ruler of Kashmir. But he did not acquire actual possession of his new province without difficulty. The governor appointed under the Sikh Government showed no disposition to hand over the province, and with the aid of feudatories attacked Gulab Singh's troops. Gulab Singh had to apply to the British Government to aid him, and British troops were accordingly sent to Jammu to enable Gulab Singh to send his Jammu troops to Kashmir, and two British officers, one of whom was the famous Sir Henry Lawrence, accompanied Gulab Singh to Srinagar. Owing to his character for oppression and avarice he was not a popular ruler, and the people did not welcome him. But with the support of the British Government he was finally able to establish his rule over Kashmir by the end of 1846, and Sir Henry Lawrence returned to Lahore.

The state of Kashmir when Gulab Singh took it over was deplorable. The Government took from two-thirds to three-quarters of the gross produce of the land—about three times as much as is now taken. The crops when cut by the cultivators were collected in stacks. One-half was taken as the regular Government share, and additional amounts were taken as perquisites of various kinds, leaving one-third or even only a quarter with the cultivators. Of this some was taken in kind and some in cash. The whole system of assessment and collection was exceedingly complicated and 174workable only in the interests of the corrupt officials; and Government held a monopoly in the sale of grain. Gulab Singh during his lifetime did very little to ameliorate this state of things. He took things as he found them and troubled little to improve them. He died in 1857, and was succeeded by his son Ranbir Singh, who rendered valuable services to Government during the Mutiny, and received, in recognition, the right to adopt from collateral branches an heir to the succession on the failure of heirs-male of Gulab Singh on whom alone the country had been conferred by the British. Maharaja Ranbir Singh died in 1885.

During his reign there was a steady improvement, but it was very slow, and an account of the condition of Kashmir then reads curiously ill beside the account of the province now after nearly a quarter of a century of the present Maharaja's reign. The Maharaja Ranbir Singh himself was extremely popular both with his people and with Europeans—in this respect being a marked contrast to his father. He was manly, fond of sport, affectionate in his family, and simple and moral in his private life. And Mr. Drew has given a pleasant picture of how this chief, 175in the old-fashioned way so liked by the people and so conducive of good relations between rulers and subjects, used to sit daily in public Durbar in full view of his people, receiving and answering his people's petitions.

AKBAR'S BRIDGE, KARALLAYAR

With the vastly more complicated system of administration of the present day it is practically impossible for a ruler of Kashmir to conduct his business on precisely these lines; but I have seen the same system working in Chitral, and quite realise the advantages it has for small states. If it does nothing else it teaches the people good manners, for they learn from observation of others how to comport themselves in high society. But these public Durbars are also an education of no small value. Here the people discuss men and events. They learn character and hear outside news, and it is surprising to see how much more native intelligence, dignity, and character men brought up in these conditions have than the school-bred men of to-day.

Ranbir Singh was then a typical ruler of a type that is now almost gone. Unfortunately he had not the officials capable of the immense labour required to remove the terrible effects of 176many centuries of misgovernment, and especially of the harsh, cruel rules of the Afghans and Sikhs. His officials were accustomed to the old style of rule and knew no better. In the early 'sixties cultivation was decreasing; the people were wretchedly poor, and in any other country their state would have been almost one of starvation and famine; justice was such that those who could pay could at any time get out of jail, while the poor lived and died there almost without hope. There were few men of respectable, and none of wealthy appearance; and there were almost prohibitive duties levied on all merchandise imported or exported. By the early 'seventies some slight improvement had taken place. The labouring classes as a general rule were well fed and well clothed, and fairly housed. Both men and women were accustomed to do hard and continuous labour, and it was obvious that they could not do this and look well unless they were well nourished. Their standard of living was not high, but they certainly had enough to eat. And this is not surprising, for a rupee would buy 80 to 100 lbs. of rice, or 12 lbs. of meat, or 60 lbs. of milk. Fruit was so plentiful that mulberries, apples, and apricots near the villages were left to rot on the ground. And 177fish near the rivers could be bought for almost nothing. Crime of all kinds was rare, chiefly because of the remembrance of the terrible punishments of Gulab Singh's time, and because of the system of fixing responsibility for undetected crime upon local officials. Drunkenness, too, was almost unknown. About half a lakh of rupees was spent upon education, and another half-lakh on repairing the "paths." A slight attempt was also made to assess the amount of land revenue at a fixed amount This much was to the good, but yet the country was still very far indeed from what it ought to have been. The means of communication were rough and rude in the extreme, so that men instead of animals had to be used as beasts of burden. Even the new assessment of the land revenue was three times as heavy as that of the amount demanded in British districts in the Punjab. And there was still much waste land which the people were unwilling to put under cultivation, because under the existing system of land revenue administration they could not be sure that they would ever receive the results of their labour. A cultivator would only produce as much as would, after payment of his revenue, provide for the actual wants of himself 178and his family, because he knew by experience that any surplus would be absorbed by rapacious underling officials. In matters of trade there were, too, still the impediments of former days. Upon every branch of commerce there was a multiplicity and weight of exactions. No product was too insignificant, and no person too poor to contribute to the State. The manufacture or production of silk, saffron, paper, tobacco, wine, and salt were all State monopolies. The sale of grain was a State monopoly, and though the State sold grain at an extraordinarily cheap rate, the officials in charge did not always sell it to the people who most required it, or in the quantity they required. Favourite and influential persons would get as much as they wanted, but often to the public the stores would be closed for weeks together, and at other times the grain was sold to each family at a rate which was supposed to be proportionate to the number of persons in the family; but the judges of the said quantity were not the persons most concerned, viz. the purchasers, but the local authorities. Private grain trade could not be openly conducted, and when the stocks in the country fell short of requirements they could not be replenished by private enterprise.179

On the manufacture of shawls parallel restrictions were placed. The wool was taxed as it entered Kashmir; the manufacturer was taxed for every workman he employed, and at various stages of the process according to the value of the fabric; and, lastly, the merchant was taxed, before he could export the goods, the enormous duty of 85 per cent *ad valorem*. Butchers, bakers, carpenters, boatmen, and even prostitutes were still taxed, and coolies who were engaged to carry loads for travellers had to give up half their earnings.

The whole country, in fact, was still in the grip of a grinding officialdom; and the officials were the remnants of a bygone, ignorant, and destructive age, when dynasties and institutions and life itself were in daily danger, when nothing was fixed and lasting, when all was liable to change and at the risk of chance, and each man had to make what he could while he could; and when, in consequence, a man of honesty and public spirit had no more chance of surviving than a baby would have in a battle.

No wonder that in 1877, when—through excess of rain which destroyed the crops—famine came 180on the land, neither were the people prepared to meet the emergency, nor were the officials capable of mitigating its effects, and direful calamity was the consequence.

In the autumn of 1877 unusual rain fell, and owing to the system of collecting the revenue in kind and dilatoriness in collection, the crop was allowed to remain in the open on the ground, and then it rotted till half of it was lost. The wheat and barley harvest of the summer of 1878 was exceedingly poor. The fruit had also suffered from long continual wet and cold, and the autumn grains, such as maize and millet, were partly destroyed by intense heat and partly devoured by the starving peasants. The following year was also unfavourable, and it was not till 1880 that normal conditions returned.

These were the causes of the scarcity of food-supply; and when this calamity, which nowadays could be confidently met, fell upon the country, it was found that people had nothing in reserve to fall back on; that the administrative machine was incapable of meeting the excessive strain; that even the will to meet it was wanting; and that corruption and obstruction impeded all measures of relief, and even forbade the starving inhabitants 181migrating to parts where food could be had. In addition, the communications were so bad that the food, so plentiful in the neighbouring province, could be imported only with the greatest difficulty.

As a result two-thirds of the population died; a number of the chief valleys were entirely deserted; whole villages lay in ruins, as beams, doors, etc., had been extracted for sale; some suburbs of Srinagar were tenantless, and the city itself was half-destroyed; trade came almost to a standstill, and consequently employment was difficult to obtain.

The test of this great calamity showed bare the glaring defects of the system the present dynasty had taken over from their uncultured predecessors, and which in their thirty years' possession of the valley they had not been able to eradicate.

During the five years which remained of the late Maharaja's reign the first important steps were taken to remedy this terrible state of affairs; the assessment of the land revenue was revised, and the cart-road into the valley was commenced. But it has been during the twenty-three years of the present Maharaja's reign that the most real progress has been made. First and foremost the land revenue has been properly assessed; it has been fixed in cash for a definite number of years, 182and the share claimed by the State has been greatly reduced. Then a first-rate cart-road up the Jhelum valley has been made. The heavy taxes on trade have been reduced. A well-trained set of officials have been introduced, and they have been well paid. Increased, though not yet nearly sufficient attention has been paid to education. Surveys for a railroad have been made, and a great scheme for draining the valley, reclaiming waste land, and preventing floods has been commenced. As a result, and in spite of the State taking a smaller share of the cultivator's produce, the revenue has more than doubled. More land is being taken up. The population is steadily increasing. The darkest days are over, and the future is assured.

The history of the people has shown that there is latent in them much ability and taste, but that they have always prospered most when most subjected to the influences of the great world outside Kashmir. Those influences are now strong upon the country, and the future prosperity of the people will very largely depend upon how they meet and profit by them.

Needless to add, a weighty responsibility lies also upon the British Government that it should guide their destinies aright.

CHAPTER X

183

ADMINISTRATION

A more detailed account of the administration may now be given. Kashmir Proper, that is, what is known as the valley of Kashmir, is a province of the Jammu and Kashmir State, which has a total area of about 80,000 square miles, and a population of 2,905,578, while the province, which includes for administrative purposes the valley of the Jhelum River from Baramula to Kohala, as well as the district of Gurais on the far side of the North Kashmir Range, has a population of 1,157,394.

Kashmir itself is administered by a Governor, and the whole State is ruled over by a Maharaja. It is one of what are known as the Native States of India,—States which are ruled by their own Chiefs, but feudatory to the British Government, whose interests are represented by a British Resident at the capital.184

The present ruler, who succeeded his father in 1885, is Maharaja Sir Pratap Singh, G.C.S.I., a major-general in the British Army, and a Chief of strong religious tendencies, who is much respected in India and loved by his own people. He is advised by a chief minister, his very capable and business-like brother, Raja Sir Amar Singh, K.C.S.I., and by three subordinate ministers—one in charge of the foreign relations of the State, of the Public Works, the Forests, and several minor departments; another in charge of the Land Revenue administration; and the third in charge of the Home Department, including the Police, the Customs, Medical and other branches. The Judiciary is presided over by a Judge of the High Court.

All of these officials are natives of India, and, except one, belong to the British service, and have been trained in British provinces. None are Kashmiris. They have been lent by the British Government to the Maharaja for a specified number of years, and draw salaries of from Rs. 1200 to Rs. 1500 a month, or £720 to £800 a year.

Under them, again, are the governors of Kashmir and of Jammu; and the wazir-i-wizarats of Ladak (including Baltistan) and Gilgit, of whom all 185except the latter are also Indian officials lent by the Government of India.

Besides these, in the departments of the State where special technical knowledge is required, European and American specialists are employed under the ministers. The finances of the State are controlled by an Accountant-General from the British service. The operations for assessing the land revenue are under a Settlement Commissioner, a member of the Indian Civil Service. The public works are under the charge of a retired engineer from the Public Works Department of the Government of India. The forests are controlled by a Conservator of Forests from the Indian Forest Department. And under the State Engineer is the Chief Engineer of the Electrical Department, a Royal Engineer Officer, who in his turn has under him a large staff of Englishmen, Americans, Canadians, engaged in carrying out the great schemes for converting water power into electric power, and by means of the latter draining the water-logged portions of the valley, reclaiming land, and preventing floods.

This, in brief outlines, is the administrative system in the State. At the head is an hereditary ruler. Immediately responsible to him are a group 186of Indian officials mostly born, educated, and trained in the adjoining British province of the Punjab. The local executive is likewise chiefly presided over by Government of India native officials; and in charge of technical departments are European and American specialists.

What is chiefly remarkable is the very small number of Kashmiris who are employed. Though the majority of the inhabitants are Mohamedans, very few Mohamedans are employed in high positions. Though the Kashmiris are very intelligent, extremely few have posts in the State service; and this anomaly, though remarkable, is paralleled in many other native States. They are most of them dependent on officials trained or at least educated in British provinces. The Maharaja of Kashmir realises, however, the necessity of educating and training his own subjects, and most of the smaller officials and many of the clerks in the offices are State subjects.

43

And these are the men with whom visitors to Kashmir come mostly in contact. Immediately under the Governor of Kashmir are officials known as tehsildars, in charge of tehsils or small districts, and under them again are naib-tehsildars in charge of groups of villages; and, finally, we come to the [187]lumberdars, or head-men of the villages. These officials with their attendants collect revenue, keep order, and administer justice in small cases. But for the administration of justice there is also in the Kashmir provinces a Chief Judge holding his court at Srinagar, and minor judges known as munsiffs.

The chief revenue is derived from the land, and is assessed according to a system which will presently be described. Out of a total revenue for the whole State of one hundred lakhs of rupees, the revenue from land amounts to over forty lakhs.

Customs is another principal source of revenue. The receipts for the Kashmir province for the last three years were—

s.	3,99,155	£26,610
s.	4,84,235	£32,282
s.	5,51,102	£36,740

and for the whole Kashmir State—

s.	7,62,582	£50,839
s.	8,93,438	£59,562
s.	10,09,647	£67,243

In describing the history of the people we have seen that one of the greatest reforms effected in the reign of the present Maharaja has been in the system of assessing and collecting the land revenue—a reform which was carried into effect mainly by [188]Sir Walter Lawrence, who in his work on Kashmir has described at length both the old system and the one which has given it place. Of every village, with its village lands, a map was made on a scale generally of 24 inches to the mile—that is large enough to show every field accurately, and even the trees on the fields. Then in the village registers all necessary facts relating to each field were recorded, such, for instance, as the area, the class of soil, the source of irrigation, the number and description of trees on it, the name of the owner, the name of the person who cultivated it, and the amount of rent payable by the tenant, if any.

Of these entries the most important, as regards assessing the amount of land revenue to be paid, was that regarding the class of soil. This is now classified as A, irrigated land, (1) producing rice regularly; (2) producing rice occasionally, but not in every year; (3) producing other crops than rice; and B, unirrigated land, (1) manured; (2) level unmanured; (3) sloping unmanured.

The name of the "owner" was entered, but "owner" is really an incorrect term, for all land in the Kashmir valley is "owned" by the State. The actual holders have a right of occupancy as against the State as long as they pay its dues, and are [189]practically sub-proprietors; but they have no right of alienation or mortgage.

At each harvest an official called a patwari, made a field to field inspection, and recorded in a Register the crops found in the fields. These proceedings gave the assessing officer a record of crops which formed an aid to assessment. The officer then estimated by observation, inquiry, and experimental cuttings, the yield of average fields of each class. The following are examples of some of the rates of yield:—

	Per Acre.	
	bs.	bs.
a. Unhusked rice—		
1. In villages affected by floods	240 o	520
2. In villages above the floods but not too near the mountains	760	600
3. In villages close to the mountains and affected by cold winds and		

cold water	360	800
b. Maize on unirrigated land—		
1. By river	200	600
2. Between river and mountains	100	500
3. Near mountains	00	200
c. Wheat on unirrigated land—		
1. By river	40	20
2. Between river and mountains	60	40
3. Near mountains	00	60

All this information furnished the basis on which the amount of revenue could be fixed. In old days 190the State claimed half the gross produce as it was stacked on the field at harvest time, and various perquisites of officials reduced the share left to the cultivator to only about one-third. Moreover, in collecting the revenue in kind there was much room for abuse and loss to both the State and the cultivator, and endless vexation. It was therefore the object of the new settlement to have the revenue paid as much as possible in cash rather than in kind, so that the occupant of a field would be able to know for certain what he would have to pay, and would not have cormorant officials hanging over his field at harvest time; and also so that the State on its side might know precisely what amount of revenue to expect in a year, and not have the trouble of collecting in kind with all its attendant risks and cost. What had to be fixed, then, was the money value of the grain which the State would otherwise have taken from the cultivator.

The settlement of this amount in the case of every single field in the whole of Kashmir was, necessarily, a gigantic operation and took six years to carry out. But the information collected regarding its area and bearing capacity showed, with considerable degree of accuracy, what each field could produce. The average cash value of this 191amount of produce in an ordinary year was then determined, and the State had then to say what proportion—whether two-thirds as before, or an half or a third—they would take. Lastly, had to be decided for how many years they would agree with the occupier to take this fixed amount of cash—whether for ever, as in Lord Cornwallis' settlement of Bengal, or for thirty, twenty, or ten years.

Mr. Lawrence, though making very great changes, had naturally to also use caution. He could not at once fix the whole revenue in cash. Some had still to be taken in kind. And he could not safely make his settlement for more than ten years, for his calculations of the produce of a field and of the money value of that produce might at this first settlement often be unfair, either to the State or the occupier.

At first even the villagers, who were most to be benefited, distrusted the settlement and hampered the operations, and the old style petty official, now happily extinct, encouraged them in their distrust. But gradually, under Mr. Lawrence's influence, the attitude of the villagers changed. When they saw that for ten years to come the amount the State was to take was to be fixed and at a diminished rate, that only a small part was to be taken in 192kind, and enough was to be left to them for food, and that thereby the ever-present sepoy was to be removed from the villages, the people began to realise that some good was to come of these operations for settling the revenue. Ruined houses and desolate gardens were restored, absentees returned, and applications for waste land came in faster than was for the time convenient.

At the end of the ten years a second settlement was made, and this time with much diminished troubling, for not only were people and officials better disposed, but there were now available much more reliable statistics as to the produce of the fields. The yield of each field and the money value of the yield could now be fairly accurately known; and the proportion of this money value of the yield which the State should take had now to be fixed. Formerly, exclusive of perquisites for local officials, the State would take half the yield. But it was now decided to take only 30 per cent of the gross yield, and to take the money value of it instead of the actual produce in kind as in old days. Each occupier was then given a small book containing a copy of the entries in which he was interested, the area of the field, the rate he had to pay, and so on.193

The all-round incidence of the new land revenue proper is Rs. 3. As. 2. (or 4s. 2d) per acre cultivated; and the rates varied from Rs. 12 (16s.) per acre on some of the less irrigated (market garden) land, to ten annas (tenpence) per acre on the poorest unirrigated land in the coldest part of the province.

The period of the settlement was fixed at fifteen years.

CHAPTER XI

PRODUCTS AND MANUFACTURES

What Kashmir is principally known for to the outside world is its shawls; but the wool from which they are manufactured is not produced in Kashmir itself: it comes from Tibet and Chinese Turkestan. It is the soft down lying under the long hair of the Tibetan goat. Kashmir does, however, produce a coarser wool of its own. Kashmir villagers keep immense numbers of sheep, for round their villages and on the mountain uplands there is an abundance of rich grass, the leaves of the willow trees and of irises furnish winter fodder, and these animals are not only thus easily fed, but also furnish their owner with clothing, with food and with manure, and by crowding in the lower portion of his house keep him warm in winter. They are shorn twice in the year, once in early summer and again in the autumn. The wool is of good quality, and in the winter months the women spin it, and the men weave it into blankets and into the well-known "puttoo" cloth, in which sportsmen in Kashmir clothe themselves, and for which, since the Swadeshi movement, there has been a great demand in India.

Silk is another and increasingly important product. The whole of the valley is covered with mulberry trees, and for many centuries sericulture has been practised in the country. But it is only recently that it has been placed on a really business-like footing. Now good "seed," *i.e.* silk-worms' eggs, are imported fresh every year from France and Italy—about six-sevenths from France and one-seventh from Italy—and in the spring are given out to the cultivators free of charge. The villagers hatch out the eggs, feed the silk-worms on the mulberry leaves, and then bring the cocoons to the State silk factory at Srinagar for sale. 1720 lbs. of eggs were given out last year, and 1,712,000 lbs. of cocoons were bought in by the State. In the present year the figures were 1762 lbs. of eggs and 2,273,760 lbs. of cocoons. The amount paid for these cocoons to 17,433 rearers was Rs. 4,25,848, so that the Kashmiri villagers at very little trouble and no cost are able to put a nice little sum of money into their pockets every summer, and are consequently now clamouring to be given seed. The mulberry trees are carefully watched by the State, and an inspector of mulberry trees goes round the valley, seeing that the trees are not damaged and are properly pruned. Young mulberry trees are distributed by the State to the villagers to the number of from 30,000 to 40,000 a year.

Fruit is another of Kashmir's important products which may be expected to largely increase in the future. Kashmir apples are renowned all over India. They are large, red, and attractive looking, and sell well as far down as Calcutta and Bombay. But they are not of really good flavour, and the apples from European stock now being grown are sure to have a large sale in the future. In the autumn months thousands of cart-loads are carried down the roads to the railway at Rawal Pindi. The apple grows wild in Kashmir, and the villagers uproot the wild trees and plant them in their orchards. But the State also now supplies them with young trees. Near Srinagar there are large State nurseries stocked with the best kinds from Europe, and every year thousands of young trees are given out free to the villagers, so that the valley may gradually be filled with the best available trees. The State also to a small extent grows apples for sale, and their trees are extraordinarily prolific. In the autumn one sees these apple trees weighed down to the ground with fruit, and M. Peychaud, the director in charge, says that he has taken as many as 30,000 from one tree. The apples also grow to an enormous size. And when the railway comes to Kashmir, and carriage is easier and cheaper, the export of apples and other fruit should increase to striking dimensions, and not only be one of the best means of making the railway pay, but bring great profits to the cultivators. The apple of Kashmir has a great future before him.

So has the pear. He is not so much to the fore at present, because he does not stand carriage as well; but the railway will remove that drawback, and he will run the apple hard. Like the apple, the pear also is found wild and transplanted into orchards. But good stock is now being grown in the State orchard and distributed from there. Some of these, and some that have been imported by European residents, have taken so kindly to Kashmir, that I believe their present products are not surpassed anywhere. From Major Wigram's garden comes a famous pear, so large, and soft, and luscious, as scarcely to support its own weight. Other winter pears keep right through to the early summer.

Quinces also are grown in considerable quantities. They make excellent jam, but are chiefly grown for their seed, which is exported to the Punjab.

Grapes have been tried, and on the shores of the Dal Lake there is a vineyard under the charge of a Frenchman, from which what is known as Kashmir wine is made. But this branch of fruit culture has not so far been so successful as the culture of pears and apples. It is said that the rain falls at the wrong time. But probably the most suitable descriptions of grapes have not yet been tried or the most suitable site yet selected. In the time of the Moghals they were plentiful, and wild vines are often seen. So it is hard to believe that grapes cannot be grown in Kashmir as well as the other fruits for which it is famous.

Walnut trees are found all over the valley, and quantities of the nuts are now exported, though formerly they were only used for oil. They are an excellent fruit, and one kind known as the *kagazi* has such a thin shell that it is easily cracked between the fingers, and the kernel is 199excellent. The villages on the lower slopes are often surrounded with walnut trees, some of enormous size, and adding greatly to the beauty of the village.

THE CAMPING-GROUND AT LIDARWA

Mulberries, as has been remarked in regard to sericulture, are plentifully grown. They are eaten in immense quantities by the people as well as by their animals.

Almonds are grown in considerable quantities in large orchards. Apricots are grown, but not very plentifully, and principally for oil. Peaches, cherries, pomegranates, and plums are also cultivated, but have not yet received much attention from the villagers. Strawberries grow abundantly in the gardens of Europeans, and gooseberries and currants also succeed. There is, indeed, scarcely a limit to what the fruit production of Kashmir might be if it received attention and care.

Of the food grains rice is the principal. With all the streams running down from the mountains ample water for the copious irrigation it requires is available. The Kashmiris are exceptionally clever in its cultivation, and they grow it up to an altitude of 7000 feet. The fields are terraced 200carefully to hold the irrigation, and are incessantly watered and anxiously weeded. Lawrence says that in one district alone he has found fifty-three varieties, and certain villages are famous for their peculiar rices. But they may be roughly divided into two classes, the white and the red, of which the former is the more esteemed by epicures, though the cultivators prefer the latter as it is less delicate, suffers less from changes of climate, and gives a larger out-turn. Lawrence gives the average crop of unhusked rice per acre as 17 maunds, or 1220 lbs. Large quantities of rice are exported to the Punjab.

Maize is the next most important crop. In the black peaty land lying along the Jhelum, and in the high villages where numbers of cattle graze and manure is plentiful, very fine crops are grown. As a rule it is grown on dry land, and is seldom irrigated. The stalk forms excellent fodder for cattle. The average yield in irrigated and dry swamp land is 11 maunds, or 880 lbs., and on dry land 8 maunds, or 640 lbs. per acre. As a diet maize ranks after rice, but the villagers, when money is scarce, will sell their rice and subsist on maize.

Barley is largely grown, but it is not of good quality, and no pains are taken in its cultivation.201

Wheat receives better treatment, but the wheat flour of Kashmir is not esteemed. The average production on dry land is 7 maunds, or 560 lbs. per acre.

Millet is another food grain grown in Kashmir, but not very generally.

Buckwheat is cultivated in the higher villages.

Pulses are not much grown. *Mung* (*Phaseolus Mungo*) is the best, and is often sown in rice lands which require a rest. Others are *raáh*(*Phaseolus radiatus*) and *mothi* (*Phaseolus aconitifolius*). Peas and white beans are occasionally cultivated; in the gardens of European residents they give excellent results.

Oil-seeds are largely grown, and now that a company for oil-pressing is being started, still more attention is likely to be paid to them. The Kashmiris do not use *ghi* (clarified butter) in their food. They consequently require vegetable oils for that purpose, and as mineral oils are too expensive, they use them also for lighting. The principal oil-seed grown is the rape, of which there are three varieties. An average crop is 3 maunds, or 240 lbs. per acre. Large quantities of linseed are also produced, of which an average crop would be 1½ to 2 maunds, 120 to 160 lbs. per acre. *Til* 202(*Sesamum indicum*) is a very common crop. It yields 1½ maunds, or 120 lbs. per acre. Til is also extracted from the walnut and apricot. Rape seed gives the best oil for lighting purposes, and linseed for eating.

Cotton is grown to a small extent all over the valley, and both the fibre is used for home-manufactured cotton cloth, and the seed is used as food for cattle.

Tobacco is cultivated in many parts. And two very beautiful crops are amaranth and saffron. The former is grown in many places along the edges of the fields, and gives a purply crimson touch to the landscape. Its minute grains are first parched, and then ground and eaten with milk or water. It is especially used by the Hindu on festival days. The latter is grown on the plateau above Pampur, and when in blossom forms one of the sights of Kashmir. The plant is like a crocus, and the flower mauve and purple. A large space of the plateau is covered with it, and this sheet of colour adds a strikingly beautiful effect to an already beautiful landscape. The saffron of Kashmir is famous for its bouquet, and is used as a condiment and as a pigment for the forehead marks of the Hindus. The flowers 203are dried in the sun, and the pollen is extracted by hand. It is this pollen and the pollen-bearing portion of the flower which form the saffron.

A WAYSIDE SHRINE

Mustard is also grown—mostly for oil; and round the town, especially round Srinagar, in the vicinity of the Dal Lake, vegetables are cultivated in market gardens. The cultivation of potatoes, indeed, is now increasing so rapidly that many scores of cart-loads are annually exported to the Punjab.

Hops are grown by the State at Dabgarh near Sopur, and their cultivation could doubtless be extended, but so far the cultivators, who are very conservative, have not taken to it.

Such are the chief vegetable products of Kashmir, and the State is making endeavours to improve existing staples and introduce anything new which may prove productive in the country. For this purpose the Maharaja has established a model farm, known as the Pratab Model Farm, and situated near the Shalimar garden to experiment with different varieties of grain and different methods of cultivation, and it is hoped that if new varieties prove specially productive they will be taken up by the cultivators. The farm was 204opened by Lord Minto in the autumn of 1906. Long rows of accurately measured plots of ground, one-sixteenth of an acre each, are planted with the different varieties, and their yield carefully measured. As one passes up the line he sees at a glance the relative qualities of each variety of wheat or maize or rice, and if the farm is carefully worked for a series of years it ought to give some valuable results. Already the cultivators have been attracted by the enormous size of some maize from Canada grown on the farm. Some very straight Russian flax recommended by the Dundee Chamber of Commerce seems to promise good results. And perhaps beetroot for sugar may also have a success, for almost any vegetable product that grows in a temperate climate will grow in Kashmir.

The crops reaped in the spring in Kashmir are wheat, barley, rape, flax, pea, and bean. Those reaped in the autumn are rice, maize, cotton, saffron, millet, tobacco, hop, amaranth, buckwheat, pulse, sesame.

The alluvial soil of the valley is of great fertility, and every year is renewed by rich silt from the mountain streams. The soil of the higher parts is 205not so rich, though it, too, will give good returns. Irrigation is largely used for water is abundant, as the snow on the mountains forms a natural reservoir stored up for the hot weather, when it melts and runs down to the valley at the time when it is most wanted. The Kashmiri is very clever at making his little water channels and leading the water on to his field.

The agricultural implements used are simple and primitive. The plough is light, for the cattle which are yoked to it are small. It is made of wood, and the ploughshare is tipped with iron. The spade likewise is made of wood, has a long handle and a narrow face, and is tipped with iron. A hand hoe is also used for weeding.

Ploughing for rice, maize, and other autumn crops commences in the middle of March. In April and May these crops are sown. In June and July wheat and barley, sown in the previous autumn, are harvested. In July and August linseed is harvested. In August and September cotton-picking commences. In September and October rice, maize, and other autumn crops are harvested. In November and December ploughing for wheat and barley takes place. And during the winter rice and maize and other autumn crops are threshed.206

FORESTS

Besides agricultural products the yield of the forests of Kashmir is also of great value. All the northward-facing slopes are covered with dense forests, a considerable part of which is of the valuable deodar. This is cut into sleepers, launched into the streams which find their way into the Jhelum, and so allowed to float down the river to the plains of the Punjab. Here the sleepers are caught where the river is slow and shallow, and sold at considerable profit to the State. The deodar is a very handsome tree, and is a variety of the cedar of Lebanon. It will be noticed by visitors to the valley along the road between Uri and Baramula, especially near Rampur. Less beautiful and less valuable as timber is the Blue pine (*Pinus excelsa*). It grows to a greater height than the deodar, which does not flourish above 6000 feet, and it may be seen at Gulmarg. The Himalayan spruce (*Picea morinda*) is very common, and also grows round Gulmarg, but its timber is of little value. Birches grow high up above the pines and next the snows; their timber is of no use, but the bark is much employed for roofing. In the forests are also found silver fir, horse-chestnut, and maple.207

All these forests are owned by the State, and are now under the charge of a Forest Department, with a conservator from the Government service at its head. The boundaries of forests are being laid down, and the State is determining under what conditions neighbouring villagers and others may be granted the customary concessions for felling timber, grazing, and gathering grass and fuel. It is usual for the State to let fuel and fodder be gathered free, and to charge for grazing and for cutting timber for building and agricultural purposes. But the areas in which these operations can be permitted, and the rates to be charged, have to be fixed, and the operations regulated. The trees are counted, marked for felling according to their age, and in regular succession, so as to allow of young trees growing up to fill their place. And in many other ways the forests are watched so as to prevent their denudation, and all the damage that would be caused through the rainfall rushing off at once instead of being held up by the trees. By the proper regulation of the forests the State raises a handsome income; it secures the soil being retained on the hill-sides; and it has the water held up in springs as a reservoir; while the authorities in the Punjab know that the rain 208which falls in Kashmir will be held up by the forests till the cold weather, when it is wanted for the canals which are taken off from the Jhelum and Chenab rivers flowing out of Kashmir territory.

Of the trees which grow in the level portions of the valley the chenar is by far the most striking. As it grows in Kashmir it is a king among trees, and in its autumn foliage is one of the many attractions which go to make Kashmir one of the supremely beautiful spots in the world. Its official botanical name is the *Platanus orientalis*, and it is one of the varieties of the plane tree. The chief characteristic is the massiveness of its foliage—its umbrageousness. It grows to a considerable height; it has long outstanding branches and great girth—one which Mr. Lawrence measured was 63 feet round the base. And as the leaves are broad and flat, the whole mass of foliage is immense, and so thick that both sun and rain are practically excluded from any one sitting in its shade. Under the chenar trees in the Residency garden one can sit through a summer day without a hat, and through a summer shower without getting wet. All this mass of foliage turned purple, claret, red, and yellow in the autumn tinting, backed against 209a clear blue sky and overhanging the glittering, placid waters of the Dal Lake or the Jhelum River, forms a picture which can be seen in no other country than Kashmir.

The elm tree of Kashmir, though not so striking as the chenar, is still a very graceful object. One in the Lolab valley has been measured as 43 feet in girth, and in the Residency garden are some fine specimens.

The walnut is more common, and round the villages many handsome trees are often seen.

The poplar is now very common, and is planted alongside the road to what is now a quite distressing extent, for though these trees give shade they also cut out the view. The timber is used a good deal for building, though it is of poor quality.

The willow is a more really useful tree, and is much planted in moist places. Its leaves are used for fodder. Its shoots are to some extent, though not sufficiently, used for basket-making.

MINERAL PRODUCTS

The mineral products of the Kashmir valley are small. In other districts of the Kashmir State there are indications of a moderate amount of 210mineral wealth. In the Jammu province there is a considerable quantity of coal of a rather poor quality, and there is good iron and bauxite. Sapphires also are found there. And in Ladak, in the Indus and its tributaries, there are gold-washings. But in the Kashmir valley, with which we are at present dealing, only a small amount of iron has been worked so far, though it is believed that large quantities exist near Sopor and about Islamabad and Pampur; and copper has also been found near Aishmakam in the Liddar valley.

Peat is extracted from the low-lying lands on the Jhelum River, and can be used as a cheap fuel. Several strong sulphur springs are found in the valley, and limestone exists in many places, notably about Rampur, and on the Manasbal Lake.

ARTS AND MANUFACTURES

Of manufactures the shawl is the best known, but the production has sadly fallen off of late years. In accordance with the treaty between the Kashmir State and the British Government, six pairs of shawls of fine quality have to be yearly paid to the latter, and but for this the industry would almost disappear. Kashmir shawls in the 211middle of the last century used to be very fashionable in Europe, but the Franco-Prussian War seems to have sealed the fate of the industry. After 1870 the fashion went out and has never revived; and the famine of 1877-79 carried off numbers of the weavers, so that now very few carry on the industry. According to M. Dauvergne, who was for many years connected with the shawl and carpet industry in Kashmir, the Kashmir shawl dates back to the times of the Emperor Baber. The first shawls which reached Europe were brought by Napoleon at the time of his campaign in Egypt as a present to the Empress Josephine.

EVENING ON THE DAL LAKE

The best shawls are made from the very fine wool, known as pashm, underlying the long hair of the Tibetan goat, which is woven into a delicate material called pashmina on which the shawl patterns are worked. Some of this pashm, and some of the best, is also imported from Chinese Turkestan from the neighbourhood of Ush Turfan. It so happens that I have been in this particular region, and I well remember the rolling grassy downs among the Tian Shan mountains on which the nomad Kirghiz kept immense flocks of sheep and goats. It was an ideal country for the growth of wool, and I believe much of this beautiful wool 212of which the finest shawls were made is now allowed to run to waste.

From 1862 to 1870 the export of shawls averaged 25 to 28 lakhs of rupees per annum, or over a quarter of a million sterling, and when the trade was at its zenith 25,000 to 28,000 persons were engaged in their manufacture.

Some of the best of the old shawls are preserved in the museum at Srinagar. They show much tasteful arrangement of colour and fineness of workmanship; but one does not wonder that they have gone out of fashion, and even at their best one misses that extreme delicacy of finish denoting strength and character in the worker which one sees in Japanese, and more still in Chinese workmanship.

Carpets have now surpassed shawls in order of importance, and two European firms, Messrs. Mitchell and Co., and Mr. Hadow, have quite as much as they can do to keep pace with the orders they receive, of which a very large number come from America. Many of the old weavers have taken to carpet-making, and the pashm used formerly for shawls is now being increasingly used for the finer kind of carpets. The dyes are good in 213Kashmir, and as the finest wool is to be had the carpet industry ought to have a good future before it.

Silk is another most thriving industry with great future possibilities. The State have now in Srinagar the largest silk factory in the world, employing about 3300 men, and turning out 191,000 lbs. of silk last year, and in the present year 230,939 lbs., most of which is sold as yarn in the European market at prices varying from 14s. 10d. to 18s. 2d. per lb., and bringing in a very handsome profit to the State. A small amount of silk weaving is also carried on in the same factory, and 212 handlooms have been set up, but at present the factory is only capable of turning out a comparatively light cloth in what is called the green state. For throwing, dyeing, and finishing, other machinery would be necessary, which the State will set up in time as funds become available. The rough cloth already made is admittedly superior to Japanese cloth of the same weight, and has sold in London at somewhat higher prices. When it can be turned out dyed and finished it should have a great sale in India, though the State are not likely to derive the same high profits from the woven cloth that they do from selling the yarn.214

Electric power has now been supplied to the silk factory from the great electric installation on the Jhelum River, and is used for heating the water in the basins in which the cocoons are immersed for reeling. It will also be used for turning some of the reeling machinery, and possibly also for electrocuting the grubs in the cocoons.

Papier-mâché is a favourite artistic product of Kashmir, and some very handsome candlesticks, bowls, and vases, well adapted for English country houses, may be purchased. The old designs are especially beautiful. But nowadays very little is made from real pulp of paper, and most of what is sold as papier-mâché is made of smooth wood.

The silver work is poor, as it lacks finish, and the modern designs are not especially beautiful. But the Kashmiri workmen used to be able to produce a peculiar sheen on the silver work which gave it a striking and unusual appearance.

Some handsome copper work is also produced in Srinagar, and some pretty enamel work.

But at present the fashion rather turns to wood-carving, which has certainly much improved since I first knew it. Very handsome screens, tables, panels, boxes, etc., are made, and the Kashmiri carpenter is getting to finish his work much better. 215Whether the work is worth the prices asked is, I think, doubtful. Better wood-carving can be had in Europe for the same price.

Turning from art industries to more practical manufactures the first to notice is basket-work. Most villages have their artisan who makes baskets for agricultural purposes, for carrying loads and for rough village work. Willow trees are plentiful and might be much more extensively grown; and Raja Sir Amar Singh has always been keenly interested in establishing a really important basket industry in Kashmir, and supplying the needs not merely of Kashmir villagers, but of India generally.

Puttoo cloth and blankets are well-known manufactures of Kashmir. Since the *Swadeshi* movement has extended in India, and the demand for goods made in India has increased, there has been a regular run on the rough woollen "puttoo" of Kashmir, and the price has gone up. Formerly a sportsman could get a good shikar suit for eight rupees. Now he has to pay ten or twelve. It is excellent wearing material, but is too loosely woven and liable to get out of shape. Proposals are on foot for establishing woollen factories in Kashmir, and with suitable machinery and proper supervision, good useful cloth should be made from the excellent wool with which the country abounds.

Cotton cloth is also manufactured in the villages, of a rough, homely description. But whether this manufacture will ever increase to a great extent is doubtful. A French gentleman who has lived for many years in Bokhara, and who visited Kashmir, told me that he considered that as cotton was grown so successfully in Bokhara and Russian Turkestan, it ought to grow equally well in Kashmir. This may be so, and the State is making experiments in cotton growing to find a variety suitable to the country. But so far the future of cotton manufacture cannot be considered so assured as that of silk and wool.

Finally, among the industries of Kashmir must be mentioned boat-building, which is indeed one of the most important in the country. The Kashmiri is an intelligent and clever carpenter, though in accordance with his character he lacks accuracy and finish. His boats are of all sizes, from the great grain barges, carrying cargoes of thirty tons, to State "parindas" or fliers propelled by forty or fifty rowers, and to light skiffs for a couple of paddlers. House-boats of quite elaborate design are also made. And if properly supervised and instructed, the Kashmiri should be capable of constructing any kind of craft.

There is little iron-work in Kashmir, for iron is not plentiful. But the Kashmiri has such natural skill that he can turn out quite good guns and rifles, and will make all the ordinary surgical instruments required in the hospital.

TRADE

Of these products and manufactures considerable quantities are exported to India, and will help to make the proposed railway pay, while this railway on its part will help to increase the exports, for much that cannot be taken out of the country, now that everything has to be carried 196 miles by road, would be exported if railway carriage were available. Apples and pears to the extent of 90,000 maunds, or 3210 tons, are exported annually, besides from 10,000 to 20,000 maunds of other fruit. Rice and maize exports vary greatly according to the demand in the Punjab. The present year was one of scarcity in the adjoining British province, and, consequently, the export of grain was quite unusual—amounting to 100,000 maunds, or more than three thousand tons; but ordinarily it does not exceed more than about a thousand tons. The export of ghi or clarified butter amounts to 720 tons. Potatoes are an increasingly important export, and the demand for them is certain to rise. Last year 750 tons were exported. Hides and skins to the amount of some 350 tons are annually exported. Linseed was in special demand last year owing to the failure of crops in the Punjab, and in consequence 1740 tons, to the value of Rs. 2,61,000, were exported; but the usual amount is only about one-fifth of this. Silk to the value of Rs. 18,44,205 was exported last year, and this may be taken as the normal amount. And wool and woollen goods, to the value of about two lakhs of rupees, are also exported, besides a few miscellaneous articles, and some 4000 live animals, mostly sheep and goats. In addition, from ten to twelve lakhs of rupees worth of timber are floated down the river.

Altogether the exports from the Kashmir valley, including timber, during the last two years have amounted to—

| 8,83,141 maunds | 31,540 tons |
| 9,77,305 maunds | 34,957 tons |

and their value has been—

Rs.	£
55,18,508	367,900
Rs.	£
49,64,800	330,986

Of this amount, deducting the timber which was floated down the river, there was exported by road—

| 1,78,355 maunds | 6,370 tons |
| 3,28,027 maunds | 11,715 tons |

Cotton piece-goods are the chief imports into Kashmir. Twenty-five to thirty thousand maunds of piece-goods (895 to 1070 tons) are imported annually, to the value of fifteen to nineteen lakhs of rupees (£100,000 to £126,000). Some are the coarse, but rough and well-wearing products of the Punjab peasants, but most are the products of Manchester, and are worn by the Srinagar and other townspeople.

Salt is the next most important import, and now that the Government of India has decreased the duty on it, the quantity imported into Kashmir is likely to steadily increase. In the last three years the amounts imported have been 112,710, 119,803, and 201,451 maunds respectively (4025, 4280, 7194 tons), with a value of Rs. 2,81,680, Rs. 4,83,698, and Rs. 5,01,485, or £18,778, £32,246, and £33,432. It is sadly needed by the poorer classes, both for themselves and for their animals, and as yet not half enough for their real requirements comes into the country. What is 220imported comes from the salt districts of the Punjab.

Tea is now being largely imported, which shows that the people are acquiring a larger purchasing power. One and a quarter million pounds of tea, with a value of seven and a half lakhs of rupees, or £50,000, are now imported annually.

Sugar is being imported in increasing quantities, the amounts for the last three years being 57,931, 62,907, and 75,817 maunds respectively, or 2070, 2246, 2709 tons, with a value of Rs. 4,58,183, Rs. 4,24,495, and Rs. 4,95,895, or £30,545, £28,305, £33,059. The Kashmiris are very fond of sugar, and as their condition improves the demand for sugar and the amount of imports is sure to increase.

Metals are another import of increasing value and importance. 20,000 maunds are annually imported, with a value of three lakhs of rupees, or £20,000. At present the Kashmiris use earthenware cooking pots, but when in time they take to metal the import of copper must increase.

Other imports of minor importance are wearing apparel, twist and yarns (of a value of nearly three lakhs, or £20,000), drugs and medicines (half a lakh of rupees), turmeric, gunny bags, leather, 221liquors, petroleum, provisions, seeds (half a lakh), manufactured silk, spices (three-quarters of a lakh), stationery, tobacco (three lakhs), and raw wool.

The total weight of imports during the last three years respectively has been—

3,35,889 maunds   11,996 tons

3,99,892 maunds   14,281 tons

4,53,202 maunds   16,185 tons

and their value has been—

Rs. 53,88,315   £ 359,221

Rs. 57,99,785   £ 386,652

Rs. 66,08,422   £ 440,561

222

CHAPTER XII

THE ELECTRICAL SCHEME

In such a country as Kashmir, with a great river flowing through it, and with numerous mountain torrents and subsidiary streams running into that river, there is obviously an immense amount of water-power at hand. The difficulty is to make it available for practical purposes. But this difficulty is now being overcome by converting the water-power into electric power, which can then be transmitted to considerable distances and applied in a variety of ways. The idea of thus converting this vast amount of water-power in Kashmir into electric power had of recent years, since the development of electrical appliances, naturally occurred to many; but it did not take definite shape till the Maharaja engaged the services of Major Alain de Lotbinière, R.E., to carry out a scheme of harnessing the waters of 223the Jhelum River which that officer had formulated, and which has just been completed.

Major de Lotbinière, a Canadian by birth, and endowed with a full measure of the energy, resource and hopefulness of his countrymen, had already executed a very successful scheme by which the water-power in the Cauvery Falls in Madras had been converted into electric energy, and transmitted to a distance of a hundred miles, to supply the Kolar gold-fields in Mysore with motive power, at a cost 50 per cent lower than that which they were paying for steam-power. He had also inspected many electrical projects on the Continent and in Canada and America. He therefore came to the work in Kashmir in September 1904 fully primed with the knowledge of all the latest developments of electrical science, and at once conceived the idea of harnessing, not any of the minor rivers of Kashmir, but the river Jhelum itself, and selected a spot a few miles above Rampur where he might entrap some of the water, lead it along the mountain-side at practically a uniform level, till he could drop it through pipes on to turbines—very much in the same manner as a mill-stream is led along and then dropped on to a water-wheel—and so by 224setting in motion various machines generate electrical energy.

The theory of the electric installation is then very simple. The valley falls rapidly. At the part selected it falls about 400 feet in 6½ miles. Some of the water is taken out and kept at about the same level so that at the end of the 6½ miles it has a fall of 401 feet. Consequently when it is dropped those 400 feet it falls with immense force and velocity. By most ingenious machinery this force is turned into electrical energy, and then transmitted by wires to wherever wanted—it is hoped even to the plains of the Punjab, to Rawal Pindi at least.

Meanwhile the water, after fulfilling its mission, returns into the river, and might, if need be, be taken out again, led along the mountain-side, and a few miles lower down dropped once more on to another electrical installation, and generate still more electrical energy. The same lot of water might, in fact, go on performing the same duty time after time till the plains of India were reached. Then when it got on to the level, and there was no further fall, it would be impossible to utilise it for generating electrical energy. But it would promptly be seized for another equally important purpose. For it would be caught in 225the great new canal which is being constructed at the point where the Jhelum River emerges from its mountain barriers and enters the plain; and from that point it would be led over some hundreds of miles to irrigate rich, but as yet uncultivated lands, only needing the touch of life-giving water to burst forth into luxuriant vegetation and attract great populations to them.

The latent capacity for good of these waters of the Jhelum, now tossing heedlessly about as they rush along beside the road into Kashmir, is then for practical purposes almost unlimited. Even the present installation only takes out a small proportion, and that portion is utilised only once. In the driest season the Jhelum River runs with a volume of about 5000 cubic feet per second—what are known for short as "cusecs." But of this amount only 500 cusecs are taken, and these 500 cusecs are utilised only once, and not several times, as they might well be in their fall between the valley of Kashmir and the plains of India.

With these 500 cusecs electrical energy to the extent of 20,000 horse-power will be generated; but Major de Lotbinière thinks that it would be possible to economically develop an aggregate of at least 250,000 horse-power of electrical energy from 226the Jhelum River. It is not possible to take out water and conduct it along the mountain-side at any point. It is indeed a matter of some difficulty to choose a site where safe headworks can be constructed to entrap the water of the river, where the water can be taken along the hill-side, and where a forebay or tank can be built from which to lead off the pipes to the generating station below. In many parts the river runs between precipitous banks so that it is impossible to get it out. In others, even when it had been got out, the hill-sides would be found so loose and unsafe it would be impracticable to take a water-course along them. Still, in spite of the many difficulties in the way of making practical use of the water-power in the Jhelum River, Major de Lotbinière still thinks that, as above mentioned, electrical energy to the extent of a quarter of a million horse-power could be economically developed.

Water for the present project has been taken out a couple of miles above Rampur at a most charming spot, where the river comes foaming down over innumerable boulders, and the banks are overshadowed by the same graceful deodar trees which clothe the mountain-sides. Here very strong and solid masonry headworks and regulating 227sluices have been built under the lee of some friendly boulders; and elaborate precautions have been taken to protect these headworks from the impact of the thousands of logs which are annually floated down the river by the Forest Department to be caught and sold in the plains below.

From these headworks what is called a flume has been constructed in which the water will run along the mountain-side to the forebay or tank immediately above the generating station. This flume, answering to the channel which conducts the water to a flour-mill, is to the eye absolutely level, but it has in reality the very small drop of 1·05 feet in 1000 feet—just sufficient to make the water run easily along it. Its length is about 6½ miles; and the main difficulty in the whole project was found in constructing it. A road or even a railway when it comes to an obstacle can very likely, by a change in the gradient, rise over it or under it. But this flume had to go straight at any obstacle in its way, for it obviously could not rise, and if it were lowered it could not rise again, and so much horse-power would have been lost at the far end. The flume, in fact, once it was started off had to take things as it found them and make the best of them. The first obstacle was a 228great spur of boulder conglomerate. This had to be cut down into to a depth of forty feet. An arched masonry passage had then to be made, and the whole covered over again.

Five torrents were negotiated by passing them clean over the flume. Over six other torrents the flume—here made of wood—had to be carried on strong iron bridges. And six tunnels were made through projecting rocky spurs. Only one-third of the 6½ miles' length of flume could be built of masonry, and the remainder had necessarily to be built of timber. This portion had an internal section of 8-1/3 feet by 8½ feet, and was constructed of tongued and grooved, machine-planed, deodar planking 2¾ inches thick, supported on cross frames 3½ feet apart.

The chief danger to guard against in constructing this flume for carrying the water to the generating station was the risk of the hill-sides either bodily slipping downward, as they are very apt to do in heavy rain, or falling in heavy masses on to the wooden flume and breaking through it, and thus completely breaking off the source of power, and bringing all machinery to a standstill. These risks cannot be entirely counteracted. In heavy rain a portion of the wooden flume may be carried away or broken. An alternative supply 229of water on occasions of exceptional rain has therefore been tapped close up to the generating station, where a strong dam has been thrown across the bed of a mountain torrent, and its waters impounded to lead through a tunnel in a rocky spur almost immediately on to the forebay. In ordinary weather there is little water in this torrent, but in heavy rain, when the flume is most likely to be damaged, it has ample water.

And although there is this alternative supply, great precautions have, nevertheless, been taken to ensure the flume against damage, and where slips are to be expected immensely solid timber shoots have been erected over it for rocks or snow and mud floods to shoot over.

On emerging from the flume the water enters the brick-lined tank or reservoir called the forebay, where it settles for a moment before descending the great iron pipe which conducts it on to the machinery in the power-house below. In this forebay there are, of course, sluice gates to regulate the flow, and shut it off altogether at one or all the pipes. And there is also a spill channel for the water to flow away to waste when it is not wanted.

Then four hundred feet below we come to the 230power-house, with all the most modern electrical plant transported from America, and much of it from the farthest western coast of America, across the Atlantic and the Indian Oceans, right across India, and then for 150 miles by road over a range 6000 feet high. The water-power made available by the flume is capable of generating 20,000 horse-power; but as that amount of power is not at present required, electrical machinery to develop not more than 5000 h.-p. has as yet been put in, though space and all arrangements have been provided in the power-house for machinery to develop 15,000 h.-p. more whenever that is required. The machinery is by the General Electric Co. of New York, and the generators supplied are of the three-phase 25-cycle type. The water-wheels upon which the water from the forebay, led down the pipes and contracted through a nozzle, impinges with such tremendous velocity that a hatchet could not cut the spout, are made of specially toughened steel, and are so cunningly designed that the utmost effect is obtained from the fall of the water, and that immediately the water has done its work it is allowed to pass away at once through a waste channel back again into the river without further impeding the machinery. These wheels 231were supplied by Abner Doble of San Francisco. They are sent revolving with immense rapidity—five hundred revolutions per minute, or eight every second—and they cause to revolve the electrical generators which are placed on the same axis, and thereby electric energy is generated. By a series of very ingenious machines this electric energy is regulated and conducted to the transmission wires which are at present carried through Baramula to Srinagar, and which will transmit the power at the extremely high voltage of 60,000 volts from the generating station to the spot where the power is required.

The carrying out of such an undertaking in a remote mountainous country, where no railway has yet penetrated and where no great industrial enterprises have yet been established, required no small amount of organising capacity, driving power, and foresight. In the spring the melting snow combined with rain, and in the summer the heavy rain brings down the mountain-sides, impedes construction progress, often filling up what has already been done, and sometimes, alas! burying workmen with it. In winter, snow and frost stopped all work. Labour difficulties were another source of trouble. Enough was not available on the spot, and many 232hundreds were engaged from distant Baltistan and Ladak, and even Afghanistan. Skilled labour had to be imported from the Punjab. With contractors other difficulties arose. They would not work without an advance of money, and when they got an advance many would decamp. Again cholera created still other difficulties, and drove labour away when it had with much persuasion been collected.

All these are no mean difficulties. They have, however, now been overcome, and this autumn the Maharaja, in the presence of many guests, opened the installation and transmitted the power to Baramula and Srinagar.

The 5000 horse-power at present available will be utilised for carrying out Mr. Field's and Major de Lotbinière's great scheme for dredging the bed of the Jhelum River and neighbouring marshes, and thus preventing floods, and for reclaiming some 60,000 acres of cultivable land. It will also be used for heating the water basins in the silk factory and turning the reeling machinery, as well as for lighting Srinagar.

When the railway which has so long been contemplated is at last constructed, more electric power will be needed. And if the Durbar in any way encourage outside enterprise, there will be 233demand for electric power for oil-crushing, for saw-mills, for wool factories, match factories, and many other purposes. In any European country or American State the whole amount of electric power would have been already sold. Similar rapidity of progress cannot be expected in Kashmir. But still we may hope that now every one can see that the electric power is there, and that it is an eminently useful product, the demand will gradually arise, and the financial success of the project be worthy of the skill and enterprise displayed by the engineers.

CHAPTER XIII

234

THE PEAKS AND MOUNTAIN RANGES

Not, indeed, from the valley itself, but from the mountains which bound it, can be seen the second highest mountain in the world, and a number of peaks of 25,000 feet and over. Kashmir is cradled amidst the very loftiest mountains, and only Nepal can claim still higher peaks.

By a fortunate coincidence the Government of India have this year published a remarkably interesting scientific treatise on the high peaks and principal mountain ranges of Asia, by Colonel Burrard, R.E., F.R.S., the officiating Surveyor-General of India, and H. H. Hayden, Superintendent in the Geological Survey of India. Both these officers have unique qualifications for the task. Colonel Burrard has for years made a special study of the Himalayas, and Mr. Hayden has for a great part of his service been engaged in investigating 235the geology of various districts of the Himalayas, and he accompanied me to Tibet.

The highest peak in the world is Mount Everest, which is taken to be 29,002 feet above sea-level, and is situated at the back of Nepal. The *second* highest is the peak K^2 situated on the boundary between the Kashmir State and Turkestan, and on the main watershed dividing the rivers of India from the rivers of Central Asia. It is 28,250 feet above the sea, and is visible from Haramokh on the northern range of Kashmir.

It may be wondered why so high a peak has no name. The reason is that, though high, it is not visible from any inhabited place. It is hidden away in a remote mountain region behind other peaks of almost as great magnitude, which being nearer overshadow it—as Mount Everest itself is overshadowed from Darjiling by the Kinchinjunga range. There is no village within six days' travel of K^2 on either side, and, consequently, until it was fixed by observation of the Survey, it was unknown. Colonel Montgomerie, when making the survey of Kashmir, discovered K^2. It was among a series of peaks on what is known as the Karakoram range, and each of these he designated by the capital letter K, after Karakoram, and by a number, 236K^1, K^2, K^3, etc. So it came about that what proved to be the second highest mountain in the world became known, not by any name, but by merely a letter and a number.

In 1887, on my way from Peking to India, I passed close under K^2 on its northern side, and in a paper read before the Royal Geographical Society in the following year made some reference to it. At the conclusion of my lecture, the late General Walker and Sir Henry Rawlinson proposed the name of Godwin Austin, after the survey officer who made the topographical survey of the southern portion of the Karakoram range. This name was adopted by the Geographical Society, and now appears on many maps. But it has never been accepted by the Government of India, and Colonel Burrard in his above-mentioned treatise now writes:—"Of all the designations suggested for the supreme peak of the Karakoram that of K^2 has now the widest vogue, and it will be in the interests of uniformity if this symbol be adopted in future to the exclusion of all others. The permanent adoption of the symbol K^2 will serve to record the interesting facts that a mountain exceeding 28,000 feet in height had not been deemed worthy of a name by the people living under its 237shades, and that its pre-eminent altitude was unsuspected until it was brought to light by trigonometrical observation."

With these observations I entirely agree.

K^2 was, as I have said, discovered by Colonel Montgomerie in 1858. He took the first observation to it from Haramokh, the conspicuous peak on the north side of the valley of Kashmir, at a distance of 137 miles. I saw it first from the north from the Aghil range which I discovered in 1887, and I subsequently passed close under it both then and in 1889, and never shall I forget the impression it left on me as I rounded a spur, and looking up a valley saw, quite unexpectedly, this real mountain monarch towering almost immediately above me, very abrupt and upstanding, and with immense masses of ice accumulated at its base. I have also seen Mount Everest from the north, and it is remarkable that both these peaks, which are so inconspicuous from the southern side, should stand out so boldly from the north. K^2 is not so massive a mountain as Kinchinjunga and Nanga Parbat. It is rather the bold culminating peak of a range.

The height of K^2 is put down as 28,250 feet above the sea. How can we be certain that this is right? The reply is that we cannot. The observations [238]have been made from immense distances, and are consequently liable to certain errors which have been discussed by Colonel Burrard.

It was observed from the following stations:—

Station.	Height above Sea.	Distance.
Shangruti	17,531	78·9
Biachuthusa	16,746	99·0
Marshala	16,906	58·6
Kastor	15,983	66·0
Thurigo	17,246	61·8
Haramokh	16,001	136·5
Kanuri-Nar	15,437	114·3
Barwai	16,304	88
Thalanka	16,830	74·7

And apart from the errors due to distance there are others which must always be counted on. As he remarks, no telescope is absolutely perfect; no level is entirely trustworthy; no instrumental graduations are strictly exact; and no observer is infallible. Then, again, the peaks themselves do not always have clearly defined summits, though K^2 happens in this respect to be a model for observation, and as it has been observed on several occasions from different stations, the errors in the mean value of height due to faults of observation are, probably, in Colonel Burrard's opinion, less than ten feet. Another source of error is the [239]adoption of possibly erroneous altitudes for the stations of observation. The altitude of K^2 was observed from Haramokh and other stations, but the altitude of Haramokh itself may be a few feet wrong, and the altitude of K^2 on this account may be thirty feet in error. Another element of uncertainty in determining the height of a peak is caused by the variation in the amount of snow on its summit. There is clearly more snow on the summit of a peak in winter than in summer, and in a hot, dry summer there may be less than in a generally cloudy, snowy summer. A more complicated description of error is introduced by the deviation of gravity from the normal in great mountain ranges. The attraction of the great mass of the Himalaya mountains and of Tibet pulls all liquids towards itself as the moon attracts the ocean. The liquid in levels on the theodolites with which observations of the peaks are made is similarly affected: the plates to the theodolites in consequence cannot be exactly adjusted, and when apparently truly levelled are in reality tilted upwards towards the mountains. At Kurseong, near Darjiling, they would be as much as 51" out of true level and at Mussouri about 37".

MOUNT HARAMOKH, FROM THE ERIN NULLAH

But the most serious source of uncertainty in [240]the measurement of the altitude of a peak is the refraction of the atmosphere. A ray of light from a peak to an observer's eye does not travel along a straight line, but assumes a curved path concave to the earth. The ray enters the observer's eye—I quote from Colonel Burrard—in a direction tangential to the curve at that point, and this is the direction in which the observer sees the peak. It makes the peak appear too high. This refraction is greatest in the morning and evening, and least in the middle of the day; it is different in summer from what it is in winter. One of the great Himalayan peaks visible from the plains of India would appear, from observations with a theodolite made to it from the plains, to fall 500 feet between sunrise and the afternoon, and to rise again 300 feet before sunset; and even in the afternoon, when it would appear lowest, it would still be too high by perhaps 700 feet. This is obviously a very fruitful source of error, and the difficulty of determining the error is increased by the fact that the curvature of the ray varies with the rarefaction of the atmosphere. In the higher altitude, when the rarefaction of the atmosphere increases, the ray assumes a less curved path. All these possible sources of error due to the rarefaction of the 241atmosphere have been most carefully studied, but even now we must allow 10 to 30 feet as possible error due to the rarefaction of the atmosphere.

A MOUNTAIN GLEN, BEFORE THE MELTING OF THE SNOWS

Summarising the possible sources of error in fixing the height of K^2 we may say the error may be from—

Errors of observation	20 ft.
Adoption of erroneous height for observing station	30 ft.
Variation of snow-level from the mean	Unknown
Deviation of gravity	Unknown
Atmospheric refraction	10 to 30 ft.

K^2, as I have said, though on the borders of the Kashmir State, and visible from the range which bounds the Kashmir valley, is not visible from the valley itself. But Nanga Parbat can be seen from near Baramula and from a few other parts of the valley, and is the most striking object in the view from Gulmarg and other points of the northward-facing slope of the Pir Panjal. It ranks eighth among the mountains of the world, except K^2 all the others being in the Nepal Himalayas. The order of the mountains is:—

	eet.
Mount Everest	9,002
K^2	8,250
Kinchinjunga	8,146
Makalu	7,790
T^{15}	6,867
Dhaulagiri	6,795
XXX	6,658
Nanga Parbat	6,620

242Being more accessible than the remote K^2 the observations for its height were made at much closer quarters, the nearest observation point being 43 miles distant instead of 61 as in the case of K^2. It was observed in all from eleven different points, of which the most remote was 133 miles. But until it had been measured by the Survey it had been marked on maps as only 19,000 feet.

Colonel Burrard says it is "the most isolated and perhaps the most imposing of all the peaks of Asia." It certainly is remarkable for its isolation. With the exception of subordinate pinnacles rising from its own buttresses, no peak within 60 miles of it attains an altitude of more than 17,000 feet. Throughout a circle of 120 miles' diameter Nanga Parbat surpasses all other summits by more than 9000 feet. And its upper 5000 feet are precipitous. It stands out therefore in solitary nobleness, and it can be seen on its northern side rising 23,000 feet from the Indus, there only 3500 above the sea. But whether it is of all mountains the really most imposing it is not easy to say, and personally I almost cling to Kinchinjunga. Rakaposhi in Hunza, which is 25,550 feet in altitude, and can be seen rising sheer up from the Hunza River 5000 feet above sea-level, is also wonderfully impressive. There is a peak on the Pamirs 25,146 feet high which can be seen rising abruptly from the plains of Turkestan, which are but a little over 3000 feet; and there is the Musherbrum Peak near K^2 which is 25,660 feet—all of which I have seen, and which I find it hard to place exactly in order of relative impressiveness. But if Nanga Parbat cannot be placed in unquestionably the first position, it will in most men's estimation approximate to it, and must in any case be reckoned among the few most striking sights in the world.

Of what are these great peaks built up? No one has yet ascended their summits, and as Mr. Hayden points out, the geologist has to do his work at close quarters, and not like the surveyor from a distance. So the composition of the highest peaks is rarely known in any detail, though the general character of the rocks can be ascertained with a fair approximation to certainty, from observation of material on the flanks, and from a distant view of the weathering character and apparent structure of the peaks themselves. From such observations it has been found that almost all the peaks of 25,000 feet or more in height are composed of granite, gneiss, and associated crystalline rocks. It had long be supposed that some of the granites found on the flanks of the great peaks which presented a foliated appearance were of sedimentary origin, and had therefore been once deposited beneath the sea. But their truly intrusive nature was recognised by the late Lieutenant-General M'Mahon, who proved conclusively that the great central gneissose rock of the Himalayas was in reality a granite crushed and foliated by pressure. It may certainly be taken that both K^2 and Nanga Parbat are composed of granite, and have been intruded or compressed upward from beneath the earth's crust.

Mr. Hayden further concludes that the exceptional height of these great peaks is due to their being composed of granite, for either the superior power of the granite to resist the atmospheric forces tending to their degradation has caused them to stand as isolated masses above surrounding areas of more easily eroded rocks, or they are areas of special elevation.

LAKE SHISHA NAG, LIDAR VALLEY

Now it is found that the axes of the great mountain ranges are also composed of granite, and it seems probable that special elevating forces have been at work to raise certain parts of their ranges above the general level of the whole. And when once such elevation has been brought about, the disparity between the higher peaks and the intervening less elevated area would undoubtedly be intensified by the destructive forces at work, for the mantle of snow and ice, while slowly carrying on its work of abrasion, would serve as a protection for the peaks against the disintegrating forces of the atmosphere, while the lower unprotected areas would be more rapidly eroded.

So argues Mr. Hayden, who further demonstrates that when, during the development of the Himalayas as a mighty mountain range vast masses of granite welled up from below, forcing their way through and lifting up the pre-existing rocks superimposed upon them, it is probable that, owing to dissimilarity of composition and to structural weaknesses in certain portions of the earth's crust, movement was more intense at some points than at others, and that the granite was raised into more or less dome-like masses standing above the general level of the growing range, and subsequently carved by the process of erosion into clusters of peaks.

The great peaks being thus of intrusive origin, the question naturally arises whether they are *still* being intruded upward; whether those great forces at work beneath the surface of the earth are still impelling them upward; and if so, whether they are being forced upward more rapidly than the atmospheric forces are wearing down their summits. From the geological standpoint Mr. Hayden says that it is not at present possible to say whether the elevatory movement is still in progress, but he adds that many phenomena observable in the Himalayas lead us to infer that local elevation has until quite recently been operative, and the numerous earthquakes still occurring with such frequency and violence forcibly remind us that the Himalayas have by no means reached a period of even comparative rest. The surveyor can as yet give us no more certain answer. Colonel Burrard says the original observations of the great peaks made between 1850 and 1860 were not sufficiently prolonged at any one station to enable us to rely with certainty on the values of the height then obtained. When a slow variation in height has to be determined it is better to carry out a long series of observations from one station only, rather than to take a number of observations from different stations, as is necessary and as was done in determining the absolute height of peaks. But in 1905 the Survey of India commenced a series of observations from one station, and it is proposed to observe the heights of several peaks for some years and at different seasons in each year. Then if a reliable series of results be once obtained, a similar set of observations can be repeated at a subsequent date, and any actual change of height that has occurred in the interval may be discovered.

DISTANT VIEW OF NANGA PARBAT FROM THE KAMRI PASS

Until these observations are made we cannot say for certain whether the great peaks are still rising.

THE MOUNTAIN RANGES

So far we have considered the isolated peaks rather than the ranges themselves. It remains to study these latter. All of them are popularly regarded as forming part of the "Himalayas." But Himalaya—pronounced with the stress on the second syllable—simply means the "abode of snow"; and geographers have had to define the separate ranges into which this great Himalayan region is divided. The name of the Great 248Himalaya is consequently reserved for the supreme range which extends from the western borders of China, carries the great peaks, Mount Everest and Kinchinjunga, and runs through Kumaon and Kashmir to Nanga Parbat, and possibly farther. This is the culminating range of the earth's surface. The range to the north, on which stands K^2 and some satellite peaks of 26,000 feet, is neither so long nor has it quite such lofty peaks. It is known as the Karakoram range because a pass called the Karakoram Pass crosses it. But a pass called the Mustagh also crosses it, and Mustagh means Ice Mountain, whereas Karakoram means black gravel. Mustagh, therefore, appears to me a much more appropriate name for this gigantic range of ice-clad mountains. It so happens that I am the only European who has crossed both passes. Each of them is close upon 19,000 feet in altitude, but the Karakoram, very curiously, has in summer no snow upon it, and the route leads over black gravel. It is a better known pass than the former, and, consequently, the name of black gravel got the start, and now this superb range of mountains is doomed for all time to suffer from this absurd nomenclature.

MOUNT KOLAHOI, LIDAR VALLEY

The range, however, lies far at the back of 249Kashmir, and it is not so much with it as with the true Himalaya range that we are here concerned. The mountain ranges which encircle the valley of Kashmir are the final prolongations of that mighty range which runs from the borders of Burma thirteen hundred miles away, and bifurcating at the Sutlej River, forms with its subsidiary spurs the cradle in which the Kashmir valley is set.

The southern branch of this bifurcation is known as the Pir Panjal range, and is that which bounds Kashmir on the south. It is the largest of all the lesser Himalayan ranges, and even at its extremity in Kashmir it carries many peaks exceeding 15,000 feet; the Tatakuti Peak, 30 miles south-west of Srinagar, 15,524 feet in height, being the most conspicuous.

The northern branch of the bifurcation at the Sutlej River of the great Himalayan range culminates in the Nun Kun peaks (23,410 feet and 23,250 feet), which stand conspicuously 3000 feet above the general crest of the range, and can be seen on clear days from Gulmarg. From near them, not far from the Zoji-la, an oblique range branches from the great Himalayan range, and constitutes the parting between the Jhelum River and the Kishenganga, the latter river draining the angle formed by the 250bifurcation. The height of this North Kashmir range, as Colonel Burrard calls it, is greatest near the point of bifurcation, one of its peaks, Haramokh (16,890 feet), reaching above the snow-line, and being the most conspicuous object which meets the eye of a traveller entering the valley from the south. Farther westward the range ramifies and declines.

The main line of the great range of the Himalayas has meanwhile continued from the remarkable depression at the Zoji Pass along by the Kamri Pass, to the immense mountain buttress of Nanga Parbat which, overhanging the deep defiles of the Indus, seems to form a fitting end to the mighty range which started on the confines of China. But there are great mountains beyond the Indus also, and whether these form a continuation of the great Himalayan axis which the river Indus would in that case have merely cut through in the gorges below Nanga Parbat, or whether the mountains west of the Indus are part of a separate range, we shall not know till these latter have been geologically examined.

CHAPTER XIV

251

THE STORY OF THE MOUNTAINS

How these peaks and mountain ranges arose is a fascinating and impressive study. It has been made by Mr. Hayden, who, in the fourth part of the scientific memoir quoted in the previous chapter, has compiled their history from his own personal investigations and the accounts of his fellow-observers in the Geological Survey of India. And surely a scientific man could have no more inspiring task than the unravelling of the past history of the mighty Himalaya. Here we have clue after clue traced down, the meaning of each extracted, and the broad general outline of the mountain's story told in all its grand impressiveness, till one sees the earth pulsating like a living being, rising and subsiding, and rising again, now sinking inward till the sea flows over the depression, then rising into continental areas, anon subsiding again beneath the waters, and finally, under titanic lateral pressure and crustal compression, corrugating into mighty folds, while vast masses of granite well up from below, force their way through, lift up the pre-existing rocks and toss themselves upward into the final climax of the great peaks which distinguish the Himalaya from every other range of mountains in the world.

For millions of years a perpetual struggle has been going on between the inherent earth forces pressing upward and the opposing forces of denudation wearing away the surface. Sometimes the internal forces are in commotion, or the contracting crust of the earth finds some weak spot and crumples upward, and the mountains win. A period of internal quiescence follows, and the rain and snow, the frost and heat, gain the victory, and wear down the proudest mountains—as they have worn away the snowy glacier mountains which once stood in Rajputana.

RAMPUR, JHELUM VALLEY ROAD

Of all this wonderful past the mountains themselves bear irrefutable evidence. Near Rampur, on the road into Kashmir, are bold cliffs of limestone, a rock which is merely the accumulation of the relics of generations of minute marine shell-fishes. These cliffs, now upturned to almost the perpendicular, must once have lain flat beneath the surface of the ocean. High up in the Sind valley, embedded in the rocks, are fossil oysters, showing that they too must once have lain beneath the sea. More telling still at Zewan, a few miles east of Srinagar, are fossils of land plants immediately below strata of rocks containing fossils of marine animals and plants, from which may be concluded that the land subsided under the sea, and was afterwards thrust up again. Again, an examination of the rocks on the Takht-i-Suliman shows that they are merely dried lava, and must have had a volcanic origin—perhaps beneath the sea. And an investigation of the rocks on the flanks of Nanga Parbat has shown that they are of granite which must have been intruded from the interior of the earth.

Everywhere there is evidence that even K^2 and Nanga Parbat lay beneath the sea, and that where now are mountains once rolled the ocean; that some once lay in soft, flat layers of mud or sand, or plant and shell deposit on the ocean bottom, while others, as the ocean bottom was upraised above the waters, were obtruded through them; and that everywhere there has been an immense pressing and crumpling of the earth's crust—a rising and subsiding, a throbbing and pulsation, which at one time has brought Kashmir in direct contact by land with Madagascar and South Africa, and at another has brought it into through communication by sea with both America and Europe; and which, finally, has projected it upward thousands of feet into the air. The evidence, moreover, shows that millions of years have passed while these titanic movements have been working out their marvellous results.

Who can but be impressed by such ages and such forces? Who that looks on those lovely Kashmir mountains, and on the mighty peaks which rise behind, and has learnt their long eventful history, can help being impressed by the immensity of time their structure betokens, by the magnitude of the movements unceasingly at work within, and by the dignity with which they yet present a front so impassive and so sublime?

IN THE SIND VALLEY

To realise the full, long-measured roll of their majestic evolution we should have to go back to the time when the swift revolving sun—itself one only among a hundred million other stars of no less magnitude—swished off from its circumference the wreath of fiery mist now called the Earth; and we should have to trace that mist, cooling and consolidating, first to a molten mass with a plastic crust enveloped in a dense and watery atmosphere, and then to a hardened surface of dry land with cavities in which the ocean settled. But the story, as it is with more detailed accuracy known, commences at the time when a shallow sea covered central and northern India, and extended over the site of the present Himalaya, including Kashmir and the region of the mighty peaks behind. This, then, is the first essential fact to lay hold of, that at the commencement of the authentic history of Kashmir, the whole—vale and mountain peak alike—lay unborn beneath the sea.

How long ago this was it is not possible to say within a million years or so. But this much may be said with certainty, that the period is to be reckoned not in thousands, nor yet in hundreds of thousands, but in millions of years. Geologists have names for different geological epochs, and do not usually speak of them by definite numbers of years, for there is still much controversy as to the precise length of time occupied by each. But to fix in the mind of the general reader a rough idea of the immense periods of time with which we are dealing in tracing the history of the mountains, it is useful to speak in terms of numbers, even though they may be only very approximately correct. We may then assume that the oldest rocks in Kashmir were deposited in sediment at the bottom of the afore-mentioned shallow sea a hundred million years ago. Some geologists and biologists think that a still longer time must have elapsed. Some physicists would maintain that even so much is not allowable. But as an average opinion, we may take a hundred million years ago as the commencement of Kashmir history.

What were the limits of the sea which then rolled over the site of Kashmir is not yet precisely known. But the lower portion of the Indian peninsula was then dry land, and connected by land with Africa; and the sea probably extended westward to Europe and eastward to China. Into it the rivers bore down the debris and detritus worked off by the rain from the dry land; and thus were slowly deposited, in the long course of many million years, sediments hundreds and thousands of feet in thickness which, subsequently upheaved and hardened, form the Kashmir mountains of the present day.

The first great movement of which authentic record has yet been traced took place at the close of the Jaunsar period. The bosom of the earth heaved restlessly, and what had already been deposited in the depths of the sea now emerged above the surface. Volcanoes burst through the crust, and the sedimentary deposits, hardened into rock, were covered with sheets of lava and volcanic ash, which now form the hills at the back of Srinagar, including the Takht-i-Suliman.

This was Kashmir's first appearance—not, however, in the form of a beautiful valley surrounded by forests and snow-capped mountains, but rather in the form of an archipelago of bare volcanic islands. And even these were not permanent, for a period of general subsidence followed and they slowly sank beneath the sea which was then probably connected with America.

During the Devonian period Kashmir was still submerged; but in a subsequent portion of the time when the Carbonaceous system was being deposited there was a second period of great volcanic activity, when the southern portion of Kashmir again formed an archipelago of volcanic islands.

Eventually all Kashmir emerged, and became part of the mainland of India at that time joined with Africa; so that Kashmir which had before been joined by sea with America was now joined by land with Africa. Such are the mighty movements of this seemingly immovable earth.

But it was only for a brief space that Kashmir was visible. Then once again, in mid-Carboniferous times, it subsided beneath the sea, there to remain for some millions of years till the early Tertiary period, four million years ago, when it again emerged, and the sea was gradually pushed back from Tibet and the adjacent Himalaya, till by the end of the Eocene period both Tibet and the whole Himalaya had finally become dry land. Kashmir was now a portion of the continental area and the culminating effort of the earth forces was at hand. For yet another period of great volcanic activity ensued, connected, perhaps, with the crustal disturbances to which the origin of the Himalaya is attributed. Masses of molten granite were extruded from beneath the earth's surface through the sedimentary deposit. And these granitic masses, issuing from the fiery interior of the earth, pushing ever upward, reached and passed the level of eternal snow till they finally settled into the line of matchless peaks now known as the Himalaya.

LAKE SHISHA NAG AT SUNSET

This then, briefly, is a record of the successive phases of upheaval and subsidence through which Kashmir has passed. Through by far the greater portion of the earth's history—through perhaps ninety out of the hundred million years—Kashmir has lain beneath the sea. And it is only within the last four million years that it has finally emerged.

What has actually caused the final upheaval; from whence came the force which raised the mountains is not yet entirely known. One well-known theory is that the earth's crust in cooling has to accommodate itself to a constantly decreasing diameter, and so gets crinkled and crumpled into folds. Anyhow from whatever cause, and quite apart from the ordinary up-and-down movements of the crust, there has evidently been immense lateral pressure, and on the drive into Kashmir many instances may be observed of the once level strata being crumpled into folds as the leaves of a book might be on being laterally pressed. There has been, says Mr. Middlemiss, "a steadily acting lateral pressure of the earth's crust tending to bank it up against the central crystalline zone [that is the core of intrusive granite of which the line of great peaks is formed] by a movement and a resistance in two opposite directions." And besides this pressure, the effect of tangential stresses tending to compress the earth's surface laterally and so form corrugations on it, there was from some remote internal cause this welling up from below of vast masses of granite which forced their way through the pre-existing rocks and formed the high peaks, the core of the Himalayan ranges.

These were the approximate causes—though the ultimate causes are not known—from which the Kashmir mountains originated. And tremendous though the forces must have been to cause such mighty effects, there is no evidence that they were violent. The stupendous result may have been imperceptibly attained. If Nanga Parbat rose not more than one inch in a month, it would have taken only 26,600 years to rise from the sea-level, and this is but a moment in the vast epochs with which we are dealing. Nature has worked without haste and without violence. Slowly, relentlessly, and uninterruptedly her work has progressed till the great final result stands before us in all its impressive majesty.

Such was the origin and history of the Kashmir mountains. It remains to trace the course of life 261upon them, and picture their appearance in the various stages of their history.

THE TANNIN GLEN, LIDAR VALLEY

In that remote time, which we have roughly taken as a hundred million years ago, when the oldest rocks, those for instance at Gulmarg, were first laid down in level soft deposit on the ocean bottom, there was no life on land or sea. In no part of the world have the rocks of this period given the slightest trace of any form of life. But in the course of time, in some warm climate and in some quarter where sea and land meet, and where, through the action of the tides, a portion of the land is alternately covered and laid open to the sunshine—that is, in some spot where earth and air, light, heat and water might all have their effect—it has been surmised that minute microscopic specks of slime must have appeared imbued with just that mysterious element which distinguishes life from all chemical combinations however complex.

Of this initial stage, which would not have been perceptible to the naked eye, no trace could possibly be left, but in the pre-Cambrian rocks in Europe there have been detected very minute specimens of the simplest known forms of life—the Protozoa—and obscure tracks and markings indicating the existence of life of some kind. And 262in the next geological period—the Cambrian and Silurian, say between thirty and fifty million years ago—there is not indeed in the Kashmir rocks yet any sign of life, but in the neighbouring district of Spiti there has been found in corresponding rocks fossils of corals, trilobites, shell-fish, worms, brachiopods (lamp-shells), and gastropods.

When Kashmir made its first brief emergence from the waters, in an archipelago of volcanic islands, though there was life of low and simple kind in the sea, on land there was none, and the islands must have been absolutely bare. Neither on hill-side nor on plain was there a speck of vegetation, not even the humblest moss or lichen, and not a sign of animal life. No bird or insect floated in the air. And over all there must have reigned a silence such as I remember in the Gobi Desert, and which was so felt that when after many weeks I arrived at an oasis, the twittering of the birds and the humming of the insects appeared as an incessant roar.

GOING TO THE WEDDING, UPPER INDUS VALLEY

It does not, however, follow from its bareness that the scenery of this archipelago may not have been beautiful, for those who have frequently passed up the Gulf of Suez know that the early 263morning and evening effects on bare deserts and rocky hills are often the most perfect in the delicacy and brilliance of their opalescent hues, and that the combination of this colouring with the bluey-green and the life and sparkle of the sea makes up a beauty which wooded mountain-sides may often lack. And as from the islands the summits of snowy ranges in India and Central Asia might be discerned, Kashmir even in its primitive and most barren stage must yet have had many a charm of its own.

But the bareness of the islands must have shortened the term of their existence, for it meant that the hills and plains were easily scoured out by the torrential rains which then fell upon them. It seems difficult in these days to imagine that when tropical rains fall on barren land they will not at once bring up a luxuriant crop of vegetation which would do much to keep the soil in its position; but in those days there was on land no plant life of any description. The hills and plains must, in consequence, have been deeply scoured, and rushing rivers have rapidly carried, in sand and boulders and muddy and chemical solution, the disintegrated surface of the land to the bottom of the sea, and laid down there the sediments and deposits which, 264subsequently upheaved, form the Kashmir rocks of the present day.

It is not until we come to the almost mediæval period corresponding to the Coal Measures, about twenty million years ago, that the record of land life in Kashmir begins.

In the hill-sides behind Khunmu, a little village about ten miles east of Srinagar, there is a series of rocks lying in layers over the older "trap" rocks of volcanic origin which form the great bulk of the neighbouring mountains, and in these sedimentary rocks, in what are called carbonaceous shales, are found some ferns named gangamopteris. They were discovered in 1906 by Mr. Hayden, and they are estimated by him to be "not younger than Upper Carboniferous," and they "may belong to the basis of that subdivision, or even to the Middle Carboniferous," that is, they may be about fifteen to eighteen million years old. At the same place, but on a layer of later date, have also been found fossil brachiopods—marine shell-fish resembling cockles—also of Upper Carboniferous times.

MOUNTAIN MISTS

This, as it happens, was an interesting period in the earth's history. For there occurred about then, 265or somewhat earlier, an extensive upheaval in many parts of the world, and mountains which have been now removed were upheaved to an altitude comparable with that of the highest ranges of the present day, and in the Punjab there then existed a snowy range with glaciers.

It was at this period that Kashmir was joined with the mainland of the Indian peninsula, which in its turn was joined with Africa, and now, at least, there must have been some vegetation and animal life. At this time of the Coal Measures—the remnants of forests growing in shallow sea-water—life was well advanced. Birds and mammals and flowers, and the more highly developed animals and plants had not yet appeared, but in the sea lived such things as star-fishes, shell-fishes, corals, sea-urchins, sea-lilies, sea-cucumbers, feather stars, sea-worms, sea-snails, cuttlefish, water-fleas and mussels, shrimps, and lobsters and fishes. In the coal swamps were ferns, "horse-tails" similar to the horse-tails of the present day, but of gigantic size, club mosses more than fifty feet high, lycopods, trees with trunks fifty feet high, and which bore catkins ripening into berries not unlike those of yews. In the fresh water were some shell-fishes, crustaceans, and fishes. On 266land were spiders, scorpions, some of gigantic size, and centipedes. Through the air flew hundreds of different kinds of insects, May flies, cockroaches, crickets, and beetles. The magnate of the vertebrate world was the labyrinthodont (traces of which have been found in Kashmir), which had a salamander-like body, a long tail, bony plates to protect his head, and armour of integumentary scales to protect his body. Of land trees and plants there were lepidodendrons with huge stems clad with linear leaves and bearing cones; huge club mosses, climbing palms, such as grow in tropical forests of the present day, great funguses, and numerous ferns.

Such was the type of vegetation and of land and sea animal life of the Coal period, and although not many remains of this age have yet been found in Kashmir, enough traces have been discovered to satisfy us that in the shallow estuarial water and on the islands of the inland sea there lived an animal and vegetable life which must have been very similar to what we know existed elsewhere.

NEAR THE KOLAHOI GLACIER, LIDAR VALLEY

For another fourteen million years or so after the Coal period there is nothing special to record in the history of Kashmir. There may have been a line of islands along the core of the present 267ranges, but the greater part of Kashmir had sunk once more beneath the waters, in which new sediments to enormous thickness were being accumulated, till in the late Cretaceous period, or about four million years ago, the great crustal compression began which finally upheaved these deposits from the ocean bottom, and formed the Kashmir of the present day. This upheaval was, however, neither sudden nor continuous. It was very gradual, it had three distinct phases, and was not complete till a million years ago when the dividing ocean entirely disappeared, and the Himalaya reached its maximum height.

And now at this period of upheaval—the Tertiary period of geologists—a great change had come in the animal and vegetable worlds. *Man* had not arisen even yet, but birds and mammals and flowers, and all kinds of trees were now developed; and this marked the threshold of the modern type of life. The ages when the great ferns and palms and yew-like conifers were the leading forms of vegetation had passed away, and the period of the hard-wood trees and evergreens had commenced. The great reptiles, too, which in such wonderful variety of type were the 268dominant animals of the earth's surface in the period following the Carboniferous now waned before the increase of the mammals.

At the commencement of the Tertiary period there grew cypress, sequoiæ (Wellingtonia and redwood trees), chestnuts, beeches, elms, poplars, hornbeam, willows, figs, planes, maples, aloes, magnolia, eucalyptus, plums, almonds and alders, laurels, yews, palms, cactus, smilax, lotus, lilies, ferns, etc. Later on appeared cedars, spurge laurel, evergreen oak, buckthorn, walnut, sumachs, myrtle, mimosa and acacia, birch, hickory, bamboos, rose laurel, tulip trees; and among flowers buttercups, marsh marigolds, chick-weed, mare's tail, dock, sorrel, pond-weed, cotton-grass, and royal ferns. Traces of all these trees and plants have not been found in Kashmir, but remains of a great many of them have been discovered, and, as it was linked on with Europe where they have been found, there is no doubt that they and the animals now to be described must have grown in the varying altitudes of the now upraised mountains.

This period, as we have seen, is particularly remarkable for the advent of mammals, and there now appeared the earliest representative of the tribe of monkeys; the ancestors of the horse, about 269the size of small ponies with three toes on each foot; herds of ancestral hornless deer and antelope; animals allied to our wolves; foxes; numerous hog-like and large tapir-like animals, some the size of elephants with the habit of a rhinoceros; opossums; and representatives of hedgehogs, squirrels, and bats. The reptiles included tortoises and turtles, crocodiles and serpents. Birds had also for some time past developed from reptiles, and now included a kind of albatross and birds allied to the buzzard, osprey, hawk, nuthatch, quail, pelican, ibis, and flamingo.

Later in the same period appeared parroquets, trogons, cranes, eagles, and grouse. And now was the reign of the hippopotamus, while there followed rhinoceros, shrew, moles, and musk rats. Later still the huge animals with probosces held the first place—the colossal mastodons and troops of elephants. The forests were also tenanted with apes. Other animals were sabre-toothed tigers and the earliest form of bear. Altogether Kashmir would at the time have been a paradise for sportsmen. But man had not yet appeared.

After the mountains had been finally upheaved it is evident, from the existence of those level 270plateaux of recent alluvial deposit called karewas, that the Kashmir valley must have been filled with a lake to some hundreds of feet higher than the present valley bottom. Where the Jhelum River at present escapes from the valley was then blocked up, and the whole valley filled with what must have been the most lovely lake in the world—twice the length and three times the width of the Lake of Geneva, and completely encircled by snowy mountains as high and higher than Mont Blanc; while in the immediately following glacial period mighty glaciers came wending down the Sind, Lidar, and other valleys, even to the very edge of the water.

LAKE SINSA NAG, LIDAR VALLEY

Whether man ever saw this lovely lake it is not yet possible to say. The Glacial period commenced rather more than a quarter of a million years ago, and it was about then that man first appeared, among other places, in the great river valleys of central and southern India, where the climate is not extreme, and wild fruits, berries, etc., were procurable at every season of the year. But when he spread up the valley of the Jhelum to Kashmir we have not yet the means of saying. What appear to be some remains of the handiwork of man were recently found by Mr. Radcliffe in a 271cave in the Lolab, near the borders of the Wular Lake, and seem to indicate the presence of man long anterior to the first dawn of Kashmir history. But the dawn of Kashmir history is only 2200 years ago, and man must have appeared 250,000 years before that. For thousands of years he must have been bravely battling against Nature and against the numerous and powerful animals which then lorded the earth. Slowly he must have made his way from the warm valleys of the Nerbudda and the Ganges to the rivers of the Punjab, and up the Jhelum valley into Kashmir. But he eventually established himself there as the beautiful lake was almost drained away and the Kashmir of the present day was finally evolved.

So we bring up the history of the mountains till it joins with the history of the people; and as the story finishes, does not one great thought emerge—the thought of the youth, the recentness of man alongside the hoary mountains? During the one hundred million years of the mountains' history mankind has existed only a quarter of a million; and his recorded history extends over not even a hundredth part of a single million years. And if we reflect on this, and consider, too, that the sun's 272heat will last to render life possible for many millions of years yet, does it not seem almost criminally childish for us—Hindus, Christians, and Mohamedans alike—to be so continually and incessantly looking backward to great and holy men of the past, as if all the best were necessarily behind, instead of sometimes looking forward to the even greater men to *come*—to the higher *species* of men who will yet evolve; of whom our holiest and our greatest are only the forerunners; and for the production of whom it should be our highest duty to consciously and of purpose pave the way, as the poor primitive men, though unconsciously, prepared the ground for the civilised men of to-day? Ought we not to more accurately adjust our sense of proportion; to rise above the ant-like attitude of mind, and attune our thoughts to the breadth and height of the mountains, to the purity of their snowy summits, and to the depth and clearness of the liquid skies they almost touch?

To some the sight of these mountain masses, the thought of the tremendous forces which gave them rise, and the idea of the aeons of time their moulding has involved, brings no other feeling than depression. The size, the titanic nature of the forces and the vastness of the time impress 273them only with a sense of the littleness of man in comparison. But why should the mountains thus depress? Why should not their history bring us the more worthy thought of the mighty possibilities of the race? For man, small in stature though he may be, is after all the flower and finish of the evolutionary process so far; he is century by century acquiring a completer mastery over Nature; and when we see how young and recent he is beside the aged mountains, when we realise how they have only evolved by minute gradations accumulating over vast periods of time, and when we reflect that nearly similar periods may yet lie before mankind, should not our thoughts dwell rather on man's future greatness and on the mighty destiny which he *himself* may shape?

With our imagination tethered to the hard-rock fact that man has developed from a savage to a Plato and a Shakespeare, from the inventor of the stone-axe to the inventor of telegraphy in the paltry quarter million years of his existence, may we not safely give it rope to wander out into the boundless future? We are still but children. We may be only as young bees, crawling over the combs of a hive, who have not yet found their wings to fly out into the sun-lit world beyond. 274Even now we suspect ourselves of possessing wing-like faculties of the mind whose use we do not know, and to which we are as yet afraid to trust. But the period of our infancy is over. The time to let ourselves go is approaching. Should we not look confidently out into the future and nerve ourselves for bold, unfettered flight?

And may we not still further hope that in the many million years the earth may yet exist we may master the depressing fate which lies before us when the sun's heat is expended; and look forward to evolving from ourselves beings of a higher order who will be independent of the used-up planet which gave them birth, and may be swarm away to some far, other sun-lit home?275

Printed in Great Britain
by Amazon